Ghost Mortem

ReGina Welling and Erin Lynn

Ghost Mortem

ISBN- 978-1095592076

Cover design by: L. Vryhof

Interior design by: L. Vryhof

http://reginawelling.com

http://erinlynnwrites.com

First Edition

Printed in the U.S.A.

Contents

CHAPTER 1

The days that change your life don't always start with a bang, but sometimes they end with one.

"Oh, baby. Yes." The purring feminine voice slid through the crack in my bedroom door and turned my insides liquid. My ears buzzed, my vision blurred, and my mind raced frantically as I tried to think of alternatives for the sounds coming from inside.

Yeah, I knew there was no better explanation, but my brain didn't want to believe what I would see on the other side of the door if I looked, and I didn't want to look.

But I did. The tiniest peek through the crack between the door, and the frame was enough. More than enough, actually.

Teeth clamping down on the inside of my cheek, I bit back a scream until it lodged in the back of my throat while my marriage shattered to pieces that fell soundlessly to the hardwood floor. Fight or flight crashed over me in a rush of adrenaline and propelled me back down the stairs.

My pulse pounding in my ears, I fled to the garage, yanked my car door open to leave, then shut it again. Running away wouldn't be as satisfying as confronting the situation head-on. Besides, I had to do something. I had to make them see how they'd hurt me. Find something to put a stop to the betrayal happening in my bedroom.

My eyes searched the depressingly empty garage and found nothing useful hanging on the barren walls.

We'd never been one of those handy couples with cabinets full of tools who could whip up a backyard arbor or bench in a weekend. We weren't sporty people, either, with bats or tennis rackets or golf clubs stashed away in cabinets. In fact, Mother Hubbard would have felt right at home in the echoing space.

Frantic with purpose, I made my way back inside, into the kitchen, and struck solid gold. Carefully and quietly, I chose and readied my weapon, settled it firmly in hand, slipped off my shoes, and crept slowly back up the stairs.

All the way down the hall, I wondered if it was weird to hope they weren't finished so that I could enjoy the looks on their faces when they saw me looming over them. Maybe. But I needed to take action, make a statement, do something epic to keep from falling apart.

Her eyes were closed, his back arched as he rose over her when I crept into the room, their noises covering mine even as I made my way closer to the bed.

My heart lurched and my vision narrowed, but I banished all traces of second thoughts and stepped closer.

A dozen phrases sprang to mind. In the end, I made only a strangled sound as I tipped the bucket and let the cold, wet shock of ice water put an end to their treachery. I couldn't have spoken anyway; my throat was too busy working with the effort to hold back sobs of pain and anger.

What? You thought I had a knife or something? Tempting, but I'm not that kind of person.

My husband rolled off his bed partner, shivered once and blinked up at me with dark, shock-glazed eyes. If I'd ever found the man handsome, I didn't anymore. He lost even more of his appeal when it wasn't shame that settled over his face, but defiance. She at least had the grace to look away and pull the sheet more snugly around her body.

I burned him with a look. Hurtful words with sharp edges tumbled through my head, none seeming strong enough to cut to the depth of his betrayal, so I bit them all back and ground out a warning, "Don't say a word. Not a single word." If I screamed now, I might never stop.

He did though. One word. "Everly." It came out flat and toneless. Not a plea or an atonement. And he still cradled her head against his chest as if to protect her from the situation when I was the one who had just been cut open and left to bleed.

"I said don't. We're over." No glib assurances would change the situation. If he bothered to try, I didn't hear him over the thrum in my ears and the booming echo in my head.

Go. Just get out. Now.

My inner voice made sense, and so I ran. Or maybe I walked or stumbled. To be honest, I'm not really sure what happened between the time I left the room and when I found myself standing in the lobby of the Fairmont Hotel, staring into my purse as if it held the secrets of the universe. The twenty-minute drive evaporated out of my head like mist burned away by the sun.

After watching me for a moment or two, the desk clerk murmured in a respectful tone, "Are you all right, Mrs. Hastings?"

Um, no. Not even a little bit. I sucked back the laugh that bubbled into my throat in case it popped out in a burst of hysteria, fumbled my debit card out, and paid for a suite.

On any other day, I'd have run to my closest friend's house for sanctuary, but since hers had been the face looking up at me from beneath my husband, that was no longer an option. Another giggle threatened at the thought, and so did tears that burned and stung.

"I'm fine." I lied and watched the clerk's lips curve into a knowing smile as he observed my lack of luggage. Excuse me for not taking time to pack when my life was falling apart. All I wanted was a dark room in a private space where I could think. Or better yet, not think. I didn't need him judging me in any case. It took more than gritting my teeth to keep from yelling at him to just hurry up and give me the key card, and more effort still to make it to the room.

As soon as I pushed the door shut with a gentle click, everything that had been building up inside me broke, and I'm ashamed to say I did, too.

If the next few hours constitute my greatest moments of weakness, then I'll own each and every minute of the time spent burrowed in the bed examining my marriage under the microscope of hindsight.

Once I knew to look for them, the signs stood out in bright neon. The little touches, the conspiratorial smiles. The way he'd put his hand on both our backs if the three of us walked into a room together.

What hurt the most was knowing she'd probably told him my every secret.

Not that I had many to keep. But let's face it, women tell each other the petty things that go on in their lives, and husbands tend to be involved in those.

What did it say about me that with time and some world class groveling, I might—maybe—have been able to consider forgiving him, but she would be dead to me forever? Probably more about my marriage than I was ready to admit at that particular moment.

Day turned to night, then to breaking dawn. I didn't sleep. Paul didn't call, and my ego took another drastic hit. Whether or not I could have forgiven him, I don't think less of myself for wanting him to ask.

Or for considering whether or not to call in sick to work.

Paul came from money. Enough that his family's philanthropic interests required a full staff to coordinate, and since he hadn't wanted me to get a job, I'd been serving as the Director of Development for the charitable arm of the business for the past few years. An unpaid position, but one I'd found fulfilling.

Until today, when working for the family of the man who had just cheated on me wasn't high on the list of things I wanted to do. But, since we were in the midst of putting on an event, I decided the homeless need not suffer because my life hit the skids.

The time to wallow had passed.

At the office, I pulled into my parking space and tried to muster up the energy to go inside.

Would anyone notice I was wearing the same clothes from the day before? Did I really care? Since the answer to both questions was the same, I had to force myself out of the car.

I could condense my day into a couple of hours of work if I delegated, and then what? Go home and deal with all that I wanted to avoid. Maybe I'd just put in the full day with overtime instead. The sofa in the break room might be comfy enough to spend the night.

Tomorrow would be time enough to file separation papers and talk to Paul about the way forward. Counseling, or divorce. We had some decisions to make.

With that not-so-happy possibility running through my head, I stepped into the lobby and pasted a fake smile on my face.

"Good morning, Albert. How did Alicia do on her placement exams?" Albert manned the building's security desk as a side job to put his daughter through college. When he didn't flash me his usual smile, I should have known something was up.

Rising, he circled the desk to put himself between me and the elevator. "I'm sorry, Everly. I can't let you go up."

Lack of sleep was probably why it took me so long to clue in. "Why? Is something wrong with the office? Should I call maintenance?"

"No Ma'am. I have my orders. I'm to tell you your services are no longer needed, and I'm sorry. Well, that last part wasn't an order, but it's true." He patted me kindly on the arm.

I, on the other hand, couldn't form words.

"It's shameful the way this is happening, but I did get them to let *me* gather up *your things*." A slight widening of his eyes went along with the emphasis on certain words. Albert was trying to tell me something, and I was too numb to understand. While I stood there trying to make sense of it all, he handed me a small box with the African violet from my desk sticking out the top.

"I really am sorry," Albert repeated and offered to carry the box to my car.

"I've got it, thanks." Back to feeling fragile, I didn't trust myself to keep from blubbering all over him. "Give Alicia my best wishes. She will do well in school; I just know it." The effort to smile cost me plenty, and when I made it back to my car, I had trouble relaxing my mouth. Pulling in a few deep breaths, I put the box in the back and slid into the driver's seat. My hand trembled so hard it took two tries to slide the key into the ignition switch.

Fired.

Cheated on and then fired. It was only 9:00 am. What next? How could my day get worse?

Just a tip from me to you. Banish that last question from your vocabulary. It can *always* get worse. In my case, worse meant getting tangled up in a murder, but at the time, I thought I'd hit the bell at the top of the lousy day scale.

It didn't occur to me until I was sitting in front of him, hardly able to comprehend what he was telling me, that consulting my husband's business attorney might not be the best idea.

"But *he's* been cheating on *me*." I figured if I repeated it enough times, Winston Durham would stop looking at me like something he'd scraped off his shoe.

He didn't, and the news went from bad to worse. By taking a night away, I'd abandoned my husband who had decided to file for divorce. What's more, he was invoking our prenuptial agreement, and other than the small sum of money my aunt had left me, I was being put out on the street with nothing but my personal items.

My Grammie Dupree had been a five-foot-nothing bundle of dynamite, and though the past few hours hadn't been any proof, she'd passed some of her fire down to me.

I flared. "I came to you for advice on how to handle a difficult situation, not to see how much money I could squeeze out of Paul on my way out the door. Yesterday I was a happily married woman, today I feel like a wrecking ball laid my life to ruins, and you're acting like I was the one running the controls."

As a boon, I was told, Paul would pay for the divorce even though he was not required to do so.

"So many young people make the mistake of signing contracts without reading them thoroughly. I can provide you with a copy of the agreement, and I've already drawn up the dissolution papers for you to sign."

I should have been surprised at how fast Paul had moved, but really, nothing could shock me anymore, except maybe if he wanted me to sign the papers in blood. Fury helped push me back from the emotional hole trying to form under my feet.

I just wanted Winston to stop talking so I could sign what I needed to sign and walk out of his office before I said something I'd regret.

But no, he droned on about things and money. All the stuff I cared nothing about. I'd gone there with the idea of initiating a trial separation while Paul and I, together, decided what to do with our marriage. According to Winston, all the decisions had been made without me, and I'd been cast as some sort of villain.

I probably should have argued more, but I'd pretty much hit my limit and needed to concentrate on the details because the landscape was getting my dander up and there wasn't a bucket of ice water handy.

Between teeth gritted hard enough to make my jaw ache, I said, "Give me the papers. I'll sign them now, pack up my car, and be out of the house by the end of the day."

A mental estimate had me leaving behind most of my fancier clothes to fit in all of my books and the only piece of furniture I owned. That was fine; I doubted I'd have a use for expensive ball gowns in my new life anyway.

I should have known there'd be another twist.

Winston didn't even have the decency to look sorry as he slid a sheaf of papers out of a folder and laid them in front of me. He'd even taken the time to attach the little flags indicating where I was supposed to sign. They fluttered as the pages landed on the desk.

"As the car was purchased and registered in Paul's name, it counts as a marital asset. You'll need to make other transportation arrangements."

Sucking back an anatomically impossible suggestion for where my freak-weasel soon-to-be ex could park the car—hopefully with his lawyer behind the wheel—I signed the papers. Glowering, I retrieved my plant from the back seat, stalked back inside, tossed the keys on the desk, and walked out of the office.

It had taken just about a half hour to strip away all but the shreds of my dignity, and leave me with a headache threatening my temples.

What was I supposed to do now?

I stood on the sidewalk contemplating that question until standing still seemed silly. My grandmother swore the Dupree women were made from sterner stuff than most, and now that I was about to go back to being one again, this was my chance to prove her right.

Winston Durham wasn't the only lawyer I knew, and he wasn't the smartest.

Resigned, I called in a favor.

CHAPTER 2

"What on earth induced you to sign this?" Patrea Heard tipped her head down and stared at my flushed face over the top of her reading glasses. "He can't be that good in bed."

That was a discussion I refused to have with someone I only knew in a professional context. "It's really as bad as Winston said?"

"Oh, honey, you've been hung out to dry. The way this is worded, he could claim half the money your aunt left you, make you pay the rest in legal fees for the divorce, and still not owe you a penny in alimony." Patrea selected the first two pages of the agreement and excused herself for a moment, taking the sheets of paper with her.

When she came back, she continued flipping through the documents, circling certain sections as she went.

"The scope of this is almost criminal. Did you read this before you signed it?" She spun a sheet for me to see and tapped the section she meant.

I sighed. "I did. Of course, I did."

Patrea tried to hide a snort behind a polite cough, and I looked again.

"Well, that part looks unfamiliar. I don't remember that section, but I must have read it because those are my initials."

Eyes narrowing in suspicion, Patrea pulled the page from me, inspected it for a moment, then pushed it back across the desk. "Look closely. Are you certain this is your handwriting?"

Obediently, I studied the loops and whorls on my signature, then picked up a pen, flipped over the sheet and wrote E.D. on the back. "Looks the same to me." I spun the paper to give her a better look.

"I'm no handwriting expert, but I know someone who is, and I'd be happy to take your ex apart in court if this is a forgery." If you've ever seen a cat poised to pounce on a mouse, you'd have recognized the look on Patrea's face.

"What would he have to gain from forging my signature? My aunt's money wouldn't cover his sushi orders for the next six months." My stress magnified the sound of Patrea's fingers drumming on the desktop.

Handwriting experts and court battles cost money—money I didn't have. Winston had made himself quite clear. If I didn't go quietly, he and the new Paul, the Paul who slept with my best friend on sheets I'd picked out, would make me pay.

Underneath all the bravado I'd generated to get through this ordeal, the scorned woman cowered and mourned her loss. Even if I could come up with the financial support to take Paul on in court, I wasn't sure I had enough fire left in me to fight. Not at that moment, anyway.

I cleared my throat and tried to sell the lie. "Listen, I signed the prenup because I was in love, and I'm not interested in taking Paul to the cleaners. That's not how I do things, and I have to live with myself when this is done."

Reaching for the page I'd penned with my initials, Patrea said, "You could always threaten to go public."

"With what?" I reached across the desk to gather up the papers and put them back in the folder while I tried to make sense of what she meant.

"Your story. There's nothing in there that prevents you from issuing a press release. Tell the public what he did to you. The family won't want the publicity, and I'm betting he'll make a fair settlement. He's the one who effectively ended the marriage, and he should pay."

I goggled at her. "I would have liked to keep my car, but I don't want his money enough to air my dirty laundry to the media. He's getting everything else; I'd like to retain a semblance of my pride. Besides, as you pointed out, I already signed the dissolution papers, so I'm not even sure why I'm here."

Probably because my life had just been shattered and scattered and abandoned to the winds of change. I needed an anchor, or better yet, someone to throw me a lifeline.

Patrea offered neither, but she did give voice to the question already pinballing around in my head. "What are you going to do now? Do you have a plan? A place to stay? I have a spare room if you need—"

I cut her off with a wave of my hand before she could finish the offer. "Thanks. I'll manage. Thank you, though." I took a deep breath, squared my shoulders and prepared to get on with the worst day of my life.

The woman behind the counter at the U-Haul rental center took one look at my face and gave me a sympathetic look. "Where you going, honey?" She waited to key in the address. The question flummoxed me. I knew I had to get out of my house. Nothing could keep me there another night, but that was as far as I'd taken the thought process.

"Home," was the only answer. "I'll go home and find a job and a place to rent." As I said it, it made the best kind of sense.

"I gotta have an address to figure up the mileage."

I gave her my parent's address. "How many days you think it'll take to get yourself settled?"

The woman was full of hard questions. "I don't know. I wasn't expecting to have to move. I'm not sure."

Her fingers danced over the keyboard. "I can cut you a deal on that one for a week." She pointed out the window toward a cargo van with the company logo splashed across the windowless sides.

"Best I can do is a hundred bucks plus taxes and mileage if you go over the three hundred allotted." Her kindness nearly undid me. "Should buy you a little time to decide where you're going."

A week. I had a week to sort out a new life. Entirely doable, right? Hey, I knew it was a long shot, but a girl has to have hope.

Ten minutes later, I settled my African violet next to my purse on the passenger's seat and fought off the urge to climb in the back and give in to the ache of misery trying to seep into my bones. My body was a dry, hollowed-out husk held together by the sheer will to move forward.

You can do this. I sat in the driveway and just stared at the house that had been my home just the day before. It seemed so alien to me now—as if it had undergone a transformation in the last twenty-four hours, and while everything might look the same, nothing was as it had been.

Should I knock? Silly when I had a key, but I still felt like a trespasser when I pushed open the door.

"Paul! Are you here?"

No reply broke the echoing emptiness. Why wasn't he standing guard to prevent me from making off with the silverware or anything else that might be construed as a marital asset? On the one hand, it could mean he didn't share Winston's view of my greedy nature. On the other, it could mean he didn't even care enough to say goodbye. Or both.

He needn't have worried; I wasn't planning on cleaning him out. I did indulge in the momentary and extremely satisfying fantasy of using the hedge clippers to make silk confetti out of his tie collection.

A quick tour of the place proved Winston had been correct in his assessment of what I'd brought to the marriage. But then, silly me, I'd believed Paul when he insisted my love was all he needed.

My leaving wouldn't make much of an impact on the decor. There was little of me in any room of the house. Not a pop of color relieved the grays and whites with which Paul chose to surround himself.

There was probably a metaphor in there somewhere, but I was too tired to look for it.

It took less than two hours to pack and when I pulled out onto the street, my back ached, and my hands were shaking on the steering wheel, but my eyes were dry. Such a paltry span of time to take apart something meant to last a lifetime, and I hadn't even called my parents to warn them I was coming home.

Chapter Three

CHAPTER 3

There's nothing better than an hour-long drive to lull one into a state of contemplation. Not at all what I needed at that particular time, so I cranked up the stereo and found a station playing classic rock. The base-model van had a scaled down interior lacking any sort of padded trim, so the music sounded tinny and strange, but it was better than silence.

Singing along distracted me from my thoughts, which was a blessing, and partway into the drive, my spirits lifted in that false sense of freedom that often follows a break-up. I didn't need Paul. I would be fine on my own. My brain scrambled to list all of his petty annoyances and the things I'd be able to do now that his opinion was no longer a factor.

Somewhere deep, I knew the inevitable emotional crash would come, but at the moment, I felt fine even if my eyes itched with fatigue. Scorching guitar solos and pounding drums set my fingers tapping on the wheel until my stomach grumbled loudly. It had been at least a day since I'd last eaten, which probably accounted for half the hollow gnawing in my belly.

Another fifteen miles rolled away under my wheels before I saw the gas station sign, and like most of the mom-and-pop stores near my hometown, the gas pumps were only there for convenience. The real money came from selling beer, subs, and pizza. This one offered a selection of fresh-baked goods and a broader menu, and diner seating in a room off to the right of the main store. There's no better balm for the soul than the scent of freshly baked bread, and my stomach clamored again as I stepped up to give my order.

"Can I get a turkey club?"

"On what kinda bread? We got white or wheat, but you can't go wrong with the rye." The woman behind the counter wore a checkered flannel over a pair of dark, men's-cut jeans and looked to be around my mother's age. Her smile was friendly while she waited for me to decide. Once she'd mentioned it, I had to choose the rye, and then she talked me into a side of fries.

"Oh no, I ..." I realized with a sense of freedom that Paul wasn't here to wag his finger at my food choices. "Yes, please." And when she offered, I opted to eat in the little dining area.

I'm one of those people who doesn't mind eating alone, and I settled on one of the padded spinning stools bolted to the floor in front of a low counter. There was no reason to take up an entire table or booth for just me.

When it came, the food was terrific. A generous portion of real turkey, not the processed deli style, between thick slices of bread with a side of fried potatoes that had never known the icy finger of a freezer. Crisp on the outside, creamy in the middle, laced with ketchup—I sighed and scarfed them down.

Because I'd chosen the first seat at the counter, my view was blocked by the wall between the dining room and the rest of the store, so I only heard the clerk refer to a perk of small-town living: the thirty-day revolving credit for known customers at a lot of the smaller stores.

"I'm sorry, but I can't do it. You have to pay your tab at the end of the month to keep it running. Thirty days and a hundred dollars is the limit. You know that."

"C' mon, you know I'm good for the money," came the response in a flirting tone followed by a short silence, and then he spoke again. "I just need another week, and I'll square up with you. I'll even toss you some extra for the inconvenience. Please, it's twenty dollars' worth of stuff, and I promise I'm good for the whole thing. Can't you just give me another week?"

Something about the man's voice sounded familiar.

After a short silence, I heard fingers tapping on cash register keys and a sigh of relief.

"I'll do it this once, but don't ask again, you hear me?" Equal parts compassion and exasperation colored her voice, but I also heard a little affection in there besides. "Now get on out of here before I change my mind."

The screen door squeaked on its hinges and clapped hard against the frame. I heard the clerk mutter something about the young scamp getting her into trouble with her boss. She was still shaking her head and looking at the door when I came around the corner, so I glanced outside.

Even through the haze of the metal mesh, I recognized the shape of his head, the cocky swagger, and the way he held his shoulders as he climbed into a jacked-up pickup with dark tinted windows.

Hudson Montayne—my second or, given recent events, maybe my third—least favorite man on the planet. What I didn't need today was a run-in with another one of my exes, not even if this one dated back to my high school days. Not even if my problem with him was mostly of my own making.

Besides, my nerves churned up again as soon as I spied the cargo van and remembered the chain of events that landed me twenty minutes from home, about to drop a bomb on my family.

"Hi Mom, I'm home." I practiced as I drove. "For good."

Yeah, nothing like being on the back side of twenty-five with a van full of nearly nothing, begging for your childhood room back. Almost made me want to keep driving, but another of my grandmother's favorite sayings came to mind: wherever you go, there you are.

If my life had turned to suck, I might as well be among family and friends while I figured out a new way forward.

There was comfort in returning to a town time forgot. Because so little had changed, it all looked familiar and somehow more real than the suburbs where I'd made my home for the past few years. Like the town had been formed from bedrock so solid it could withstand a storm and remain whole. Exactly what I needed right then.

Out of habit, I pulled my foot off the gas pedal and let the van slow down to the twenty-five-mile-an-hour speed limit just before I passed the grocery store. At this time of day, Ernie Polk usually had his cruiser tucked into the hidey-hole between the loading dock and Joe Parnell's bait shop.

Nine times out of ten, he'd be doing the crossword puzzle instead of clocking traffic, and I'd always been able to flirt my way out of a ticket, but I didn't have the patience for it now. And let's face it, I wasn't looking my best. Probably wasn't smelling too great, either. Not after all the packing and carting around of boxes.

Like always, I noticed the fluttering shreds of an old bikini top hanging off the power wires running along the left-hand side of the street. In the official story, Joe Parnell the younger had nicked Nadine Johnson's bathing suit out of her bag and tossed the top up there to prove he could throw it that far. He came off looking like a scamp, and Nadine saved her reputation.

In the true version, tanked on half a bottle of cheap wine, Nadine had stripped off her top to prove the town was so dull she could run down the main drag topless on a weeknight without anyone noticing. She'd been right, by the way.

Young Joe had stolen the top from where she dropped it, stuck a rock in one of the cups, and used it in a misguided attempt at making a slingshot. On the third swing, he let go at the wrong time, and the rest was history. The kind that turned to legend in a small town.

The morning after graduation, Nadine had packed up her little red Toyota, blown out of town, and never looked back. Last I heard, she'd landed an agent and was modeling at fashion week in NYC.

My own exit hadn't been nearly as dramatic, and I was hoping to keep my return on the low-key side as well, but I didn't hold out much hope. Rolling up in a moving van was bound to draw more attention than I wanted.

Still, circling the block twice smacked of avoidance, and that was another thing my Grammie Dupree despised. Better to get it over with and admit my failure no matter how sour the words would taste in my mouth.

This time, instead of passing the house, I pulled in behind a two-tone vintage pickup truck I didn't recognize, and hoped the butterflies in my stomach would settle in for a landing. Pink and purple petunias spilled from hanging baskets on the porch of the craftsman-style house. Cheerful colors against the slate gray paint.

Old Blue barked up a storm in his capacity as an early warning system, and the front door swung open before I had both feet on the ground.

"Everly? What a lovely surprise." My mother greeted me warmly and made an effort to keep her curiosity in check, but her gaze took in the van and every little detail of my appearance. Including, I'm sure, the slight puffiness and telltale redness still rimming my eyes. The woman never missed a trick. Or a chance to weigh in on my choices, but she had a way of settling me down with nothing more than her presence.

"Did we know you were coming today?"

"No, I should have called ahead. I'm sorry." I hugged her, held on for a moment. It took an effort of will to let go and not dissolve into a puddle of misery right there on the porch floor. I let her lead me inside.

"Dad's home from work, right? I have news, and I'd rather tell it just the one time."

The day already felt like it had stretched into two, and my watch said it was barely time to start cooking supper. All I wanted to do was drop the bomb and then crawl into bed in my old room and sleep for a week.

Mom eyed the U-Haul van, and I knew she'd probably already figured out what happened but would let me get to the explanation in my own time. If I'd been paying attention, I might have realized she had news of her own. In my defense, I was sleep deprived and wrapped up in my own problems.

"He's out in his workshop." I followed her inside, where the comfort and safety of home laid enough balm over some of the raw places I could take a breath that didn't feel like it would break my sternum.

As it always did when I walked into my childhood home, my gaze tracked to the touchstones of familiarity: photos on the mantel, mother's snow globes, a few of Grammie Dupree's bells, and the hundreds of books lining the built-in shelves.

Paul had hated every single thing about this house—the stained wood, the saturated colors my mother chose for the walls, the variety of patterns on pillows and throws. Too much warmth for his spartan tastes. I should have seen the signs, but I'd tried hard not to look.

"Did I hear someone pull in?" Dad smiled the way he always did when his eyes fell on my mom, and she returned the favor. Almost thirty years together and they still lit up in each other's presence. That was the benchmark, to me, of how a marriage ought to be. He noticed me and his grin widened. "There's my girl."

My dad's hugs are like warm blankets on a cold night. He pulled me in and patted my back before dropping a kiss on my cheek. "To what do we owe the pleasure of an unexpected visit?" A look passed between him and my mom that should have pinged on my radar but didn't because I was too busy trying to form words.

"Sit down. I have something to tell you both." I perched on the edge of the chair, my back muscles stiff and aching from the strain of carrying my failure into the house. Now that the moment was on me, there was no stopping the tears.

"You're scaring me," Mom said. Her hand fumbled for Dad's as if she needed his touch for strength.

"I'm getting a divorce." When the words finally came out, relief drained the tension from my shoulders, and they bowed until I huddled in the chair.

To fill the silence that fell after my admission, I elaborated. "Paul was unfaithful. It's over."

Mild-mannered to a fault, my father called Paul a few names I'd never heard him use before. His anger on my behalf helped drained off the nerves and brought the first small but genuine smile to my face since the nightmare had begun.

I turned to mom and waited for the inevitable. She sighed, "I hate to say it, but I did warn you about throwing away your education to marry that playboy."

"Paul is not a playboy. He runs the manufacturing arm of the family business." And now she'd made me defend the jerk. Honestly.

Talking to the wall would have been more productive. "You should have stayed in school. You'd have earned a masters by now. An accomplishment to be proud of." The implication being that the end of my marriage was not.

On that point, we wholeheartedly agreed, but it hadn't been my choice to make.

Underneath the I told you so, I knew my mother wanted the best for me. Or at least what she thought was best for me. Those rare occasions when we disagreed on what that entailed were the main times we came into conflict and being of similar personalities; we sparked fireworks off each other.

None so bright or fierce as when I had announced my engagement.

I hadn't made it halfway through my three-year bachelor's program before I met Paul. Six months later, I was a wife and a college dropout living in a large home in the suburbs, doing volunteer work to occupy my time. Mother had not been pleased.

Paul's reasons for insisting I leave school had seemed valid enough when we were planning the wedding. I realized the speciousness of them now that it was too late.

"You'll go back," she declared. "It's not too late to apply for next fall." She went on with a list of things I would need to do, and in defense of my fragile emotional state, I admit I tuned out most of what she said and looked at my dad.

"If it's okay with you, I'd like to stay here for a week." Just until the rental ran out on the van. I'd be settled into my own place by then. "While I look for an apartment."

I'd expected him to say yes and welcome me with open arms. Instead, his face fell and took my stomach along for the ride.

"Oh, Evvie, I wish you could, but we've uh … well, here it is. We've taken in a boarder. He's staying in your room."

Okay, the words I knew, but in that order, they made no sense. "You're renting my room to a stranger? Do you need money? Are you guys okay?"

Dad waved my concern away. "We're fine. It's nothing to do with money, and he's not a stranger. Do you remember my buddy, Dan Barrington?"

It took a minute to dredge the connection up from my addled brain. "The guy you met in Boy Scouts and stayed friends with, right? From Vermont. We went to his house once when I was little." I rubbed my fingers over the nubby fabric on the arm of the chair and avoided looking at my mom while I tried to pull snippets of that visit from my memory.

"He lived on a farm. There were horses, cows, a couple of kids. I can't remember their names, but we jumped in the hay, and the boy put a frog down my back."

"If I promise never to do that again, will you forgive me?" A deep voice startled me and, putting the pieces together, I turned to confront David Barrington, the man who was about to make me homeless for the second time in the same day.

CHAPTER 4

While I searched my memory for anything I might have done to deserve such lousy karma, David waited for an answer.

"Of course. I'm sorry." I rose and offered him my hand. "Everly Has … um, Dupree. It's good to see you again," I lied right to his face, and he could tell because I was too tired and emotionally drained to hide the whole of my disdain.

Turning to my mother, I said, "Could you come outside with me? I need to speak to you privately."

She followed me to the van and settled into the passenger seat. "Before you ask, I'll say that this was all your father's idea. He feels he owes a debt to Dan and giving David a place to stay was a way to repay it in some small part. David's been through a rough time, and in our defense, we had no idea there were problems in your marriage."

Her tone carried both an apology and a hint of accusation.

"Well, neither did I until I came home yesterday and found him in bed with my former best friend."

While she might be something of a control freak and annoyed me at times, I never doubted my mother loved me, or that, given a chance, she'd have gone to town on my soon-to-be ex. I'd seen her verbally strip the hide off a man before, and I almost regretted not letting her have her way with Paul.

"I'll clean out the sewing room. I'm sure we can fit a small bed in there."

Not with some strange man wandering around the house.

"No, Mom. I'll get a room at the Bide-A-Way for a week. It shouldn't take me longer than that to find an apartment and a job." After all, I knew plenty of people in town. Total piece of cake. "Tell Daddy I'll come by again soon, okay?"

"At least stay for supper." She reached over and squeezed my hand where it rested on the steering wheel.

"Thanks, but no. I'm not up to being good company. The Blue Moon is still open late, right? If I get hungry later, I'll pop in for a bite. It's all going to work out." I wasn't sure if it was her I needed to convince or me.

The knots at the end of my rope were frayed, frazzled, and too tattered to hold my weight, which is why it took so long to trip my suspicions when the motel clerk offered me a ridiculously low rate for a week's stay.

Squinting through the haze of exhaustion, I thought she looked familiar.

"You play canasta with my mother, don't you? Admit it, she called and asked you to give me the friends and family discount." I wasn't complaining, because it meant Mom cared, but I could have done without my business becoming fodder for the gossip mill.

Oh, who was I kidding? I'd driven through town in a moving van. The mill was already turning, and the only question now was how finely it would grind me up before it spit me out. Couldn't be worse than what Paul had done to me, so I gladly paid for the week, and accepted the look of pity that came with the key.

"It's offseason for another week or so," the woman said, offering me a smile. "Not even your mother could talk me into that kind of a deal once the tourists start rolling in."

I'm pretty sure she was hinting I needed to be gone by then. "Grab an ice bucket from the shelf if you want one. There's an ice maker, a couple of vending machines, and a coin-op washer and dryer in the room with the dark green door. I lock up at ten sharp so plan accordingly."

The number on the house-shaped fob went to the last door of the seven rooms—three on the left side of the office, four on the right. I pulled into a parking spot next to a blue sedan with a dented-up front fender and a bumper sticker advertising the owner had no life because his kid played basketball.

Hoping that kid wasn't planning to play ball in the next room, I surveyed my temporary home. The doors were painted with cheerful candy-colored pastels, each door a different hue, and flanked by matching window boxes. Combined, they gave the place a family-friendly appeal.

The room was clean, I'll say that much for it, but it boasted decor right out of a magazine ad from the seventies. Daisies in pumpkin orange and yellow ocher cavorted across a chocolate background of the wallpaper and clashed with the nubby textured bedspread in olive green. Paul would have hated every little thing about the place, but after my eyes adjusted to the riot of pattern, the room grew on me.

I tossed my purse on the nightstand, cranked up the AC, and fell face first onto the surprisingly comfortable bed. Because night comes late in the summer, full darkness was still a couple of hours away when I slid into an exhausted, dreamless sleep without even bothering to unpack. A sleep that was rudely interrupted just before midnight by the unmistakable sound of a headboard knocking against the wall in the room next door.

Groaning, I searched for something to throw at the wall, and since there was nothing but a lamp bolted to the nightstand and a Bible in the drawer, I chose my pillow. And while it flew across the room, there was no satisfying thump when it landed. Worse, the second pillow was too soft to sleep on, so I had to get out of bed and retrieve the one I'd thrown.

Once up and moving, I realized the room had gone chilly, but I was too sleep-addled to change the temperature again. With another groan, I crawled under the covers and dragged them over my head to tune out the noise.

Sleep came harder the second time, and when I finally fell, I dreamed of people staring at me with sad faces and talking in solemn tones.

Sunlight speared through the gap between the drapes to fall across my face at what turned out to be six o'clock the next morning but felt like the crack of dawn. With the light tickling my lids, I woke with only a vague notion of where I was until everything came back in a rush. I'd slept nearly ten hours, and as much as I might want to escape back into dreamland, there were things I needed to do.

I rose and confronted myself in the mirror over the bathroom sink. Hair sticking up every which way, eyes crusted with gunk, and crease marks on my cheek—I looked like twenty pounds of crap in a ten-pound bag. A shower and some serious makeup were in order if I was going to find a job and a place to live. I could do this, right?

Well, it wasn't like I had a choice, so I figured I'd better get moving.

All of my clothes were still in the van, so I wet my hands and ran them through my hair until it resembled a damp bird's nest—which was an improvement. For the first time in two days, it seemed luck was on my side when I managed to grab what I needed without running into anyone who might be scarred for life by the sight of me.

Some part of my brain noticed the truck parked next to the U-Haul van but was too bleary to remember why it looked familiar. Half an hour later, when the heated spray of the shower had blown away most of the cobwebs, the truck was gone, and by the time I got to Mabel's Blue Moon Diner, I'd forgotten all about it.

If not for the sign mounted on a pole in the near corner of the parking lot, you'd be hard-pressed to recognize Mabel's as a place of business. It looked more like a double-wide modular home someone had plunked down in the middle of town. I stepped through the front door that was painted a screaming red and just stood there for a moment while the mingled scents of breakfast washed over me.

Four years of marriage to a man who wouldn't be caught dead in a place like this had not adjusted my palette to his taste for small bites artistically arranged on a plate. Mabel didn't bother with pretension and would have gleefully tossed him out the door if he'd dared criticize her choice of garnish—a slice of lemon on a leaf of curly kale adorned every plate. Standing just a shade over six feet tall and built like her daddy was a refrigerator and her momma had ties to Wonder Woman's tribe, Mabel tolerated no disrespect in her place of business.

On my way to an open booth, I grabbed the local paper to look at the want ads while I ate, but didn't bother with a menu. Mabel's loaded omelet with a side of home fries had been on the menu since she opened and was my idea of the ultimate comfort food.

"Everly, I'd heard you were in town." I laid the paper aside and looked up at the familiar, smiling face of Jacy Wade, or rather, Jacy Dean now that she was married.

Did she know? Was she looking at me with pity or speculation?

The better question was: why was I being such a fool? Jacy was my oldest friend. Even if she'd heard about my unfortunate break-up, she wasn't the type to revel in someone else's misfortune — especially not mine.

I rapped my knee on the table as I rose to exchange a hug, then she held me at arm's length. "There you are. I've missed that face." She pulled me in close again, and since it was there, I breathed in the honey-and-floral scent of the cologne she'd been using since ninth grade—the year her grandmother deemed her old enough for such things.

"Still rocking that Sweet Honesty." It felt good to smile and to be smiled upon in return.

"My signature scent to the last drop."

It felt even better to giggle at the shared memory.

Based on a rumor that the cologne was being discontinued, and convinced the bottles would eventually become collector's items, Jacy's grandmother ordered cases of the stuff. Enough, she said, to get rich off her investment. She'd sworn off Avon entirely when the rumor had proven false, but from then on, Jacy received a bottle at every holiday—and I mean every single one, including Columbus Day and Fourth of July.

"When I die at the ripe old age of a hundred and ten, my kids will put the last five bottles in my casket just to make sure I have enough for the afterlife."

"And when you meet up with your grandmother on the streets of gold, you'll give her a spritz for old time's sake." I giggled again as I filled in the rest of the vow she'd made years ago.

Jacy scribbled something on her menu pad and pulled off the top sheet. "Let me put your order in, and I'll take my break so we can catch up." That last she tossed over her shoulder as she rounded the counter to hang the order on a revolving rack. She said something to Mabel in a low enough voice I couldn't make out what it was, and on her way back, grabbed the pot of hot water and a couple of tea bags.

"I don't get to order?" I couldn't help but smile in Jacy's presence.

"Pfft." She settled her trim body into the seat across from me, and with economical movements, made us each a cup of tea. "Some people drown their sorrows in alcohol, some in sweets. You always go for the loaded."

"I'm that predictable?" But she'd confirmed the rumors were already flying. "How did you know I'd need solace?"

Leaning back, Jacy shot me a raised eyebrow. "You drove through town in a moving van that was then spotted at the Bide-A-Way motel. Didn't take much of a leap to figure out something happened. If you hadn't shown up here today, I'd have come knocking on your door with ice cream and a bottle of wine later. Just in case you wanted to indulge in a little omelet-free consolation."

"It would have been good wine, right? Not that rotgut stuff we swiped from under your mom's sink when we were sixteen." I shuddered at the memory, and Jacy laughed.

"No, my tastes have improved considerably. As I remember, that was cooking wine and more than halfway to the vinegar stage, besides. I've never been that sick again in my life."

Mabel dinged the bell to announce my order was ready, and Jacy scrambled up to grab two plates. "Figured I'd eat with you. Now, tell me what happened. The real story."

The first bite of vegetable-flecked egg hit my stomach and spread warmth like a blessing for the troubled soul.

"Not much to tell. I caught him in bed with another woman." No one needed to know how close a friend she'd been since that was insult added to injury.

"You caught him? Like right in the middle of—" Instead of saying the word sex, Jacy used a hand gesture.

My blood rushed down to my feet at the memory. "Yeah, right in the middle."

Without pity, Jacy sympathized. "That's horrible, Ev. I'm sorry. Are you okay? Can I do anything?"

Anyone else might have fished for every detail, but Jacy was more concerned about me than a salacious story. Her concern untied some of the knotted tension I'd carried for the past two days.

"I've missed you, Jacy. I really have."

"What are you going to do now? Are you moving back home?" She eyed me with hope.

I sighed. "That's the plan. I thought I would stay with my folks for a week or so while I made other arrangements, but …"

"But they're renting your room out to that David guy, so you ended up at the Bide-A-Way where … never mind." She dropped eye contact and gave her eggs some undue attention.

"Where what? If there's something hinky going on out there, I'd like to know about it. Isn't it a safe place anymore?" My mother wasn't prone to gossip, but you'd think she'd have told me if there was a reason why I shouldn't be staying there.

With a funny look on her face, Jacy waved my concerns aside and gulped down a mouthful of tea to buy some time. "Nothing like that, it's just … well, Hudson's staying there at the moment and I figured, you know, with your history, it might be awkward."

Now I remembered where I'd seen that truck before, and I didn't think it was merely a coincidence that had landed me in the room next to his. Resisting the urge to bang my head on the table took more effort than you'd have thought possible.

"I'm a good person. You think so, right? So why is karma out to get me all of a sudden?"

She might not have pried into the dirty details of my imploding marriage, but Jacy was practically bouncing in her seat with eagerness to tell me what she knew of my former boyfriend's current situation.

"There was a scandal at the high school. No one knows exactly what happened, but he got demoted from head coach to assistant, and I heard even that's only on a trial basis. Then a few weeks ago, he moved out of his house and took a room at the motel."

It looked like I wasn't the only one whose life had hit the skids, but that didn't mean I wanted to start a club with him or anything.

"Thanks for the heads up. I'll try to avoid running into him."

Her break ending, Jacy reached for my plate, stacked it on top of hers, and slid out of the booth. "You'd think after all these years, he'd let it go." She referred to the grudge Hudson had held in my honor ever since I'd broken things off with him before leaving for college.

"I slapped his ego, but he'll have to find a way to move on now that I'm going to be living here again. Speaking of which, do you know if Leo Hanson still owns Brookside apartments? I need a place to live."

Jacy looked at her watch. "He does, and if you hang around another few minutes, he'll be in for his daily cup of coffee. He's here like clockwork." She grinned and lowered her voice to a conspiratorial whisper. "Not for the cup of Joe, either. He comes in to make eyes at Mabel."

Even if he were wearing boots with heels, Leo would have to stretch his neck if he didn't want to be looking Mabel's boobs right in the eye, and if he weighed anything over a buck fifty, I'd be shocked. An unlikelier looking couple might never exist. "He's set his sights high, hasn't he? Does she like him back?"

"Oh, you know Mabel. Dating doesn't rate high on her list of priorities. Or anywhere on it, really. I'm glad you're back. We have a lot of catching up to do." Without waiting for me to answer, Jacy leaned down and gave me a one-armed hug. "Breakfast is on me, and I'll see you later," she promised, then bustled off to clear and reset one of the other tables.

Keeping an eye on the door, I opened the paper to the classifieds and scanned through the limited options in the help-wanted section. I wasn't qualified for anything in the health industry or interested in a management position that was a euphemism for direct sales. You can call them floor maintenance systems all you want, but they're still vacuum cleaners, and selling them in any capacity was not my thing.

Thankful for Jacy's warning, I ruled out the substitute teacher position at the local high school where I'd be almost guaranteed to run into Hudson every day, too.

I'd given up on finding anything when Leo walked in and chose a seat where, if he leaned a little to the left, he could see into the kitchen. Watching him do just that, I knew Jacy had nailed it, but then, she'd always been able to spot a possible love connection from fifty paces.

As he picked up his cup and took a sip, his eyes tracked Mabel's every move. If I didn't know he was painfully shy and completely harmless, he'd have given me the creepy stalker vibe. Except there was a sweet hopefulness to him that made me feel sad for them both. The one who might never know love and the one determined it wasn't for her.

He's better off, the bitter and scorned part of me insisted. They both were.

“Excuse me, Mr. Hanson. May I?” I pointed to the chair opposite him at the table. Behind thick glasses, his eyes widened, but he nodded cordially enough and made polite conversation by asking after my parents.

"They're doing very well, thank you. The reason I'm bothering you is I'm moving back to town, and I need a place to live, so I was wondering if you had any apartments available." Leo owned a pair of four up/four down units on the edge of town.

"I have a three bedroom vacant now, and there will be a two-bedroom at the end of the month."

I couldn’t wait that long, so I asked for more details on the three, and then nearly fell off my chair when he named the dollar amount I’d need to move in. First, last, and security deposit would eat half my nest egg, and then he dashed my hopes entirely.

“We do require a background check and income verification.” The background check was a no-brainer, but I didn’t even have a job, so the income verification put me out of the running. “Would you like to fill out an application?”

“Okay, thanks.” My shoulders slumped. “I’m still looking for work, so I’ll have to wait unless you’d be willing to waive the income requirements.”

He had the grace to look uncomfortable when he politely explained he’d turned over the day-to-day operations to a mortgage broker who also ran a management company, and that some guy named Spencer was now calling the shots.

“You might want to visit his office anyway. I understand he’s looking to hire an assistant.” Leo gave me Spencer’s number, and I turned to leave him to his coffee and mooning, but he called after me. “You know, you could stop in at the town office. There’s a bulletin board where property owners post rental listings. I used to find a lot of my renters that way.”

“Thanks, Leo, I’ll do that.”

CHAPTER 5

"I'm sorry, but I'm not sure what I can do for you, Everly."

I smoothed down the lapel of my lucky suit while I listened to the woman behind the desk of the job agency list off the reasons she considered me fundamentally unsuitable for anything she had to offer.

"You have no real job history and no degree." She tapped a few keys, stared at the computer screen, then pinned me with a look. "Volunteer work is nice and all, but much like being the head cheerleader in high school, it doesn't carry much weight around here."

My head came up. "How do you know I was a cheerleader? I didn't put it on my application." I might have been new to the job-seeking world, but I'd like to think I wasn't that big of an idiot. I searched her face for signs of familiarity and came up empty. She had one of those desktop signs that said her name was Carlene Nicholson. Didn't ring a bell.

"You don't remember me, but then, why should you? I wasn't part of the popular crowd."

Clearly, she remembered me, and not in a good light, either.

"Look, Carlene, if I did or said something that offended you when we were kids, I'm truly sorry."

Her eyes bored into mine like truth-seeking lasers.

"Thank you for that, but it doesn't change anything." I couldn't tell by the look on her face if she'd accepted my apology or not, but Carlene's eyes raked over me, and I wondered if I was overdressed.

"Have you considered going back to school to finish your degree?"

Taking a breath, I steeled myself and said, "School isn't an option because I can't afford to go. I'm in the process of getting a divorce, and I need a job now. Anything to cover living expenses, so can you please check again? There must be something."

A hint of a smirk slid over Carlene's sly face and, knowing she wasn't going to help me, I mentally retracted my apology.

Hers rang hollow. "I'm sorry, Everly. There's nothing I can do for you. Come back when you've got more job experience, and we'll see."

My face pinked as I slid my purse strap over my shoulder. "How am I supposed to get job experience if no one will hire me?"

Carlene shrugged but declined to answer, and I walked out of her office feeling lower than an ant's undercarriage.

And that was the high point of my morning. By noon, I'd burned my way through town racking up rejections left and right. I couldn't even score an interview since no one was hiring.

By the time I dialed his number, the mortgage broker was my only hope.

Spencer Charles sounded impatient when he answered the phone, and also somewhat surprised when I asked about the position.

"I hadn't even written up an ad for the job yet. How did you hear I was looking for help?" I told him. Maybe it boded well for me to be on the ball, or perhaps I came off as pushy. Either way, I needed a job and asked if we could meet that afternoon.

He paused and then sighed. "There's a little wiggle room in my schedule. Be in my office at twelve-thirty and bring a resume."

A beat passed while I stifled my eagerness. "Of course, Mr. Charles. That will be fine."

"Call me Spencer, and what did you say your name was again?" I supplied it. "Well, Everly," he said, "be here at two, and be prepared to wait if my one o'clock runs long."

It sounded like the delay would be inevitable, and I also got the impression I shouldn't pin my hopes on landing the job if I didn't stick around until whenever he was ready to talk to me. Good enough. Tenacity was one of my strong suits even if my mother preferred the word stubborn. Sometimes it's all about the words you use.

"See you then, Spencer."

Tenacious though I might be, the idea of putting myself out there and being found wanting again sent a nervous chill over my skin. A woman can take only so many rejections in a day.

For a moment, the enormity of change threatened to overwhelm me. Two days before, I'd been on a stable, solid path in my life. Marriage, work that might not pay but was certainly fulfilling, and the promise of a family. A future I'd wanted, and had never expected would evaporate faster than a drop of water on hot pavement.

Suck it up. Sometimes my inner voice sounds like my grandmother talking to me. *You're a Dupree, and that means something.*

Tartly, I answered back, well it didn't mean enough to keep me from landing in this mess, now did it?

But the mental conversation distracted me from following the dark thoughts down a winding path, so I did my best to suck it up and move on with what needed doing. A job, a place to live, and a car being the biggest priorities.

Since I had a lead on the first, it was time to see what I could do about the second, so I fired up the van and headed to the other end of town to find out if Leo's advice held any water.

Housed in what had once been the elementary school, the town office was only open three days a week, and I counted my lucky stars I'd shown up on one of them. I stepped into a vestibule with shelves and a line of coat hooks running at child height down either side. From there I went through a steel door with a horizontal lever for a handle and chicken wire between the panes of safety glass.

Inside, marks and patched-in spaces on the floor showed where classroom walls had been removed to make space for a waiting area on the one side of the long counter. Behind the currently empty reception area, some of the classrooms had been converted into office space, some into storage for old records according to ceiling-mounted signs.

The place smelled as if chalk dust had settled into long forgotten corners and lingered to rise up and tickle the nose with its dry, powdery scent. I held back a sneeze and checked each wall for the bulletin board. Leo hadn't lied, exactly, but he hadn't prepared me for the sheer volume of papers tacked one over the other and littered with a rainbow of sticky notes.

My heart sank as I scanned for the newest addition to the board: a two-year-old poster for a Halloween party. Leo probably hadn't been in here since he turned over his property management to Spencer Charles. Or worse, there just wasn't anything to rent.

Even with the generous discount I was getting at the Bide-A-Way, staying there wasn't a permanent solution. If things kept up this way, I'd end up living in a yurt in my parents' back yard. Shudder.

I scanned the message board again in the vain hope I'd missed something the first time around and had just about decided I was totally out of luck when a door snicked shut in the back of the building and footsteps clicked my way.

"I'm sorry, I didn't hear you come in. I have the bidding form right here." Before I could dredge up the woman's name because I recognized her as another friend of my mother's, she'd slapped two sheets of paper down on the countertop and was looking at me warily. "Deadline's one pm." It was twelve thirty when she handed me the pen.

"For what?" I asked, confused. "I think you're mistaking me for someone else. My name's Everly Ha—Dupree." I'd have to get in the habit of using my maiden name again. "And you're Mrs. Tipton." My memory finally supplied a name to go with the kindly face.

"Oh, my lands. Of course! You're Kitty's girl."

Martha Tipton plucked a pair of glasses, held by a cord around her neck, from where they lay on her ample bosom. She put them on and gave me an up and down look.

"I'm sorry. I thought you were that vulture who—" She drummed her fingers on the laminated surface, and from the way her tone lowered, I got the impression she was about to drop some private information on me. "Imagine wanting to tear down the old Willowby place. It's a town landmark, it is."

I knew the house she meant.

"I'd like to know how she found out we were ready to put it up for bids. We like to give our own folk the first chance at a tax foreclosure before we resort to a public sale. Especially when it's a place that has some history. The title wasn't supposed to transfer until Thursday, and then we'd have had most of a month to arrange a private sale before putting it up for public auction. There was a snafu at the title office, and we lost our window."

She'd thrown me a lot of information to process all at once, but I seized on the most pertinent. "Someone wants to tear down Spooky Manor?" Using the term didn't earn me any points with Mrs. Tipton, but when I was growing up, every kid in town knew the place was haunted.

"Now you listen to me, Everly Dupree," she said, drawing her painted-on eyebrows down and wagging a finger at me. "There's nothing wrong with that house. It belonged to Mrs. Willowby, and she lived there alone until she had to go to a nursing home just a week shy of her ninety-third birthday. Died a month later, must be a little over a year ago. Now, I ask you, would an elderly woman really choose to live alone for fifty years if her house was haunted?"

Suitably chastised, I allowed she probably wouldn't, and Mrs. Tipton let out a triumphant harrumph sound. "We stalled on the foreclosure in hopes someone from her family would come forward and claim her property, but no one ever did."

Because it's spooky and haunted. I kept the thought to myself because saying it out loud would invite wrath.

"Just between you and me, a person from town could have the place and everything in it for next to nothing, but I made out like we were in the middle of a bidding war and it would cost a pretty penny when that woman called about putting in a bid. Said she was from some investment corporation." Looking at the grim set to her features, I figured Mrs. Tipton for one of those women who'd bash a mouse to death and smile while she did it.

She'd worked herself into quite a state. "What's an investment corporation doing sniffing around here, I ask you. I think someone in the title office has a case of loose lip-itis. We don't need no outta staters coming in here and trying to take over the town."

I'd heard variations of that refrain before, and it was a popular sentiment based on plenty of past experience. City and suburban people were drawn to small towns like ours for an extended visit, and who could blame them? Despite the brutal winters, Maine is known as Vacationland.

Tourism provides good revenue, so while visitors are welcome, the trouble comes when some decide they like the slow and easy pace of small-town living so much they just have to relocate. At first, they're eager to settle in and enjoy the lifestyle, but it never lasts.

Before long, the transplants begin with the condescending digs about the town's political structure being backward, and how it's up to them to get involved so they can show the simple folks how it should be done. You'd think they were on a divine mission to bring the town up to date. Left unchecked, they'd take away all the charm that had drawn them there, to begin with.

Curious, I had to ask. "How much is next to nothing, and what do you mean by everything in it?"

Whispering, she named a figure right around half of what Leo had wanted for first, last, and security deposit. "Place could use a little cosmetic work, but the bones are good, and the mechanics were all updated in the last ten years. As far as the contents, whatever is on the property goes with it. The good, the bad, and the ugly. It's a *take one, take all* type thing."

"So I'd own the house outright?" I heard a voice in the back of my head muttering about things that looked too good to be true, and told it to shut up and leave me alone.

"The taxes would go up some because you'd lose the elderly exemption and the one for residents who have lived in the home more than a year, but that one would be reapplied on the next cycle." She tapped some numbers into a calculator, checked them against a book she pulled from under the counter, then keyed in a few more before showing me the total. "That's a ballpark, and I figured it a little high. You'd need to pay the amount in arrears and the estimated taxes for the first year up front."

The total would be less than Leo's quote on an apartment and still leave more than half the money in my account. She hit me with an estimate for insurance and utilities, but even then, I could swing it with a minimum-wage job. Talk about taking off some pressure.

I didn't even think twice, though I probably should have. I picked up the pen, filled out the bidding sheet, and added a couple of hundred to the number she'd named just because I couldn't live with myself if I paid so little for an actual house. Her eyes danced when I handed in my bid with twenty minutes left on the clock, and she clapped her wrinkled hands in delight.

"I need a certified check for the funds. Hurry now, you have just time enough to get to the bank and back before the deadline."

It took almost the entire twenty even though the bank was close by. Breathless, I gave a little smile of triumph and handed Mrs. Tipton the check with a minute to spare.

“Be a day, maybe a couple before we can put the paperwork through to transfer the deed, which takes another day to file, but it looks like you’ve just bought yourself a house.”

Dazed, I listened to her explain what would happen next, accepted the card she pressed into my hand with the office number, and walked out the door. I’d just bought a spooky old house, and I couldn’t stop smiling. There had to be something wrong with me.

Ten minutes to two, I pulled into a space in front of the mortgage broker’s office and sucked in a breath to calm the sudden flutter of nerves in my belly. If this went well, I could cross another major thing off my list. One week to get my life back on track? Try one day. Piece of cake.

Wrapping that attitude around me, I sailed through the door.

"Everly Dupree." I gave the woman manning the small reception area my most charming smile, and for once I didn't stumble over the name. "I have an appointment with Spencer Charles."

I expected her to give me a job application, but instead, she jerked her head toward the closed door on my right. “Go on in.”

Even sitting down, I could tell Spencer was a tall man. And that he had lousy manners because he didn't bother with either greeting or pleasantries. Instead, he scanned me from head to toe and reached out, his hand palm up.

Lost for what he might want, I stood still for a beat, and he snapped his fingers impatiently. “Resume. I need to see your job history. Don’t tell me you forgot. That doesn’t bode well for you, does it, Ms. Dupree?”

He hadn't invited me to sit, but I did so anyway. The interview was not going well, and it hadn't even really begun.

“I probably should have mentioned this, but I don’t have a formal resume. This would be my first paying job.”

He looked at me like I was a specimen in a bottle. “Look, I need someone with organizational skills and administrative experience. I don’t have time to train a bored housewife.”

Cross all manner of social skills off his repertoire, too.

CHAPTER 6

My chin went up. “I’m not bored, and I’m not a housewife. You need someone with administrative experience? I spent the last few years heading up a not-for-profit foundation where I coordinated a series of projects that raised several million dollars for various charities. It was an unpaid position.”

“Then why didn’t you put that on a resume?” He asked in a dry tone, and a heated blush prickled over my face.

I already knew I’d blown the interview, so just to make sure I burned the bridge right down to the cement piers, I stood and didn’t bother to censor myself while I over-shared.

“Because until now, I’ve never needed a resume, and there hasn’t been time to research what to put on one since I’m in the middle of the worst week in my life. And Carlene told me my history wasn’t valid because she hates me for something I don’t even remember doing. But anyway, thank you for your time. I’ll be sure to rectify the oversight.”

Whirling, I marched out the door before the stinging in the back of my throat gave way to a scream of frustration or a bout of tears. Either was possible. Spencer Charles might be a jerk, but I’d been completely unprepared and then turned into a raving lunatic.

One of those things I could fix before my next job interview. The other was not my problem.

I’ve always considered myself a glass-half-full kind of a person, but my ego was still smarting when I pulled into the parking lot of the local library. Built from brick with the low-slung roof, clean lines, and metal columns common in the 1950s, the place had always been like a second home to me.

Inside the door, I stopped to inhale the familiar scent of musty old leather, paper, and ink. When I also caught a whiff of adhesive, I detoured to the office and leaned against the door frame to watch the fascinating process of repairing a book. With flying fingers, the head librarian stitched together the set of signatures stacked in the sewing frame.

"Nice job, Mom." I strolled over and gently flipped over the cover she would soon attach to the assembled pages. She'd replicated the original, which lay nearby for reference, right down to the texture on the leather. "You do such beautiful work." My compliment was an honest one, for my folks had instilled a love of books in me at an early age. To see the painstaking attention to detail in her restorations filled me with pride. The work was a labor of love and artistry.

“Thank you, darling.” The final stitch finished, she snipped the thread with a tiny pair of scissors, then looked up at me. “David has offered to move out and let you have your old room back.” I couldn’t tell if the prospect relieved or worried her, but it didn’t matter.

“There’s no need. I’ve … um … well, I’ve found a place to live.” There would be a lecture when I told her what I’d done, I knew, but I stiffened my spine and spilled the story anyway.

To my surprise, she grinned at me. “Your grandmother would be so proud.”

“Which one?” I knew Grammie Dupree would have thrown me a party for doing something so outrageous, but I had no idea what my maternal grandmother might have thought. Most of what I knew about her came from looking at pictures in the family photo albums. She’d been the kind of woman who never smiled for the camera.

Whether she was pleasant when the spotlight was off, I couldn’t say, but since my mother rarely spoke of her, I suspected the stern expression to be habitual.

Mom smiled at me. "Both of them, now that I'm thinking about it, if for different reasons." As much as I would have liked to know more, she didn't elaborate. "It's a big house, but well-built with solid bones, and in a good location. With some cosmetic updates, it will be an excellent investment. Interest rates are destabilizing the market right now, so it would be best if you held onto it until things settle."

My mouth opened, but nothing came out.

“What? I know things.”

"I never doubted it. I just thought you'd disapprove. To be honest, I've been wondering if I did the right thing. I got caught up in the excitement, and Mrs. Tipton kept throwing numbers at me. I don't even have a job yet, and that's another thing. I need a resume. My head is just spinning. And don't you think it's weird that the town would let that house go so cheap? She said some investment company was interested and I'm betting they would have paid a lot more."

I could hear myself babbling as I settled into a straight-backed chair, but lacked the control to stick to a train of thought or better yet, just shut up.

"Everyone says the place is haunted, and hey, I bet that's why it was so cheap. I bet there was no investment company at all, and Mrs. Tipton took advantage of me. She talked me into buying Spooky Manor, and now I have to live by myself in a haunted house."

Wisely, my mother let me talk until I ran down like a wind-up doll because she knew me well enough to know I processed things in my own weird way.

“Rent-free.” A tentative smile slid over my face as I circled back around to the reason I’d bought a house without even seeing the inside of it first. Maybe the ghosts would be good company. Or they’d facilitate my slide into madness. You never knew.

Seeing I was done, my mother picked up the conversation as though my little meltdown had been full of valid information. “Have you ever seen a ghost hanging around the Willowby house?”

“Of course not.” Probably because I’d always walked on the opposite side of the street if my path took me down Lilac Lane. “None of my friends did, either.” Now I was starting to wonder if I’d let a case of the childhood frights turn into more.

"No one ever has,” Mom said, examining the finished book to make sure she’d gotten it just right. “These are the kinds of stories you hear, and they always start with someone's cousin or a friend of a friend who heard it from someone who heard it from someone else."

I rested my elbow on the table and my chin in my palm while I thought back. “You’re right. Okay, then if the house isn’t haunted, it makes even less sense for the town to let it go for peanuts.”

Her steady brown eyes met mine. "Does it? Isn't fear of a thing often more terrifying than the thing itself? The power of suggestion is a strong force."

I let her half-convince me, but I still thought there was something hinky with the whole scenario.

She sighed and said, "It's a solid house that you could flip, or better yet, would be a good place to raise a family if you don't mind putting in a little hard work."

"Mom, I'm in the process of getting divorced. The last thing on my mind at the moment is raising a family. You get that, right?" The idea of dating actually made the thought of living with ghosts more palatable.

Seriously, what did that say about my life?

She played off the gaffe. "I wasn't suggesting you jump on the first man who looks at you sideways, but you'll heal and move on eventually."

The question I'd held inside for the better part of two days finally popped out. "How could Paul do what he did, Mom? Why didn't he love me enough to be faithful? Why wasn't I enough for him?"

"Oh, Everly. Darling, the only answer I have for you is that there's something fundamentally wrong with the man." When I started to protest, she held up a finger. "No, don't give me that look. You know I never could find a way to bond with Paul, but I was willing to accept him as long as he made you happy. Was he good to you?"

Rising, she came around the desk to pull me up and into her arms. I laid my head on her shoulder and tried to remember my life before the enormity of the moment when everything fell to ruin.

Looking back from here, I could see the frayed edges in our marriage that I hadn't noticed from the inside. Being brutally honest, I'd let him take charge, not because he made me feel threatened if I didn't, but because it was easier to coast along with him in the lead. The part of me that hadn't felt fulfilled went ignored—first from a sense of compromise and later, just from habit. There had been nothing abusive in our marriage, not like my mother was thinking anyway.

"Mostly. I guess. Not like you and daddy, but the two of you are freaks of nature."

A watery chuckle followed that bit of truth out of my mouth. I offered another. "We were talking about trying."

"Trying?"

"To have a baby. I wanted so badly to start a family, and now that dream is over."

Stepping back from the hug, Mom laid her hands on my cheeks and turned my face until our eyes met. "Take the time you need to heal, but don't throw away all your dreams over a man who wasn't worthy of the least of them. Do you hear me?"

I nodded and let the conversation die. It was easier to let her think a happy marriage might still be in my future than to dash her hopes. I was through with men. Period. Forever. End of story.

"If I'm going to move on with my life, I need to find a job so I can afford to keep my haunted house and support the ghosts in style. Do you mind if I use the computer in here? My laptop is still packed in a box, but I need to put together a resume and print a few copies."

"Of course, honey. You know the password." Mom patted my hand and went back to her project while I searched the Internet for a resume template, then set to work making myself look good on paper. To be honest, I wasn't feeling so hot about my off-paper attributes at the moment.

I'd have bet good money I wasn't the first scorned woman to turn the magnifying glass around and search for things she had or hadn't done that might have caused such a rift. Oh, I knew I wasn't responsible for his decision to cheat, but there had to have been a few steps between him saying I do and then deciding to do it with someone else.

And that was who she was to me now—someone else—because she'd clearly never been the friend I'd thought she was. Double the betrayal, double the heartbreak.

"Everly, dear. Do you need help?" Mom's voice startled me out of the rabbit hole my thoughts had taken me down. "You've been staring at the screen for several minutes now."

So much for letting her think I'd grown a spine.

Hastily, I hit print and a copy of the single sheet representing my accomplishments and suitability for a job. Pathetic. "I'm fine. What do you think?"

She scanned once, then twice, and then nudged me out of the chair.

“Not bad, but you could strengthen the description of your duties. It’s okay to toot your own horn once in a while. That’s what a resume is for.” Fingers tapping the keys, she added and refined, then hit print. “That’s better.”

Sheets in hand, I leaned down to give her a kiss on the top of the head.

“Come for dinner tonight,” she urged. “I’ll do lemon chicken. You know it’s one of your favorites.” It was, and I was on the verge of saying yes when she added, “David likes it, too.”

Partway to the door, I turned back. “He’ll be there?”

“Of course he will. He’s a *nice* young man, Everly.” The emphasis on nice was a dig at Paul.

Maybe so, but I didn’t want him crammed down my throat. “I almost forgot. I made plans with Jacy tonight. Sort of a girl's night in, so can we do it another night? I'm home for good now. There'll be plenty of chances." Her face fell, and I rushed to add, "Better yet, give me the recipe, and you can be my first dinner guests when I'm settled into the new house. Well, after the ghosts, of course."

While she smiled, I could tell she was disappointed, because there were still little frown lines marring her forehead. “That would be lovely, dear.”

CHAPTER 7

Even in the most populated section of town, houses weren't stuffed into lots so tiny a person could reach out their bedroom window and slap the neighbor's siding. Small-town folk prefer more breathing room than that.

My new home sprawled across the left-hand side of over a quarter acre of uncut lawn.

I never claimed to be sensitive or psychic or to have any woo-woo tendencies at all, but the palpable displeasure rising up in me at the sight of such neglect might have been Mrs. Willowby's almost as much as my own.

"I'll get the grass cut first thing." My mutter must have pleased her, or my curiosity drove away the fanciful notion because when I ascended the porch to take a peek in the windows, it was with anticipation. Anticipation that quickly turned to annoyance because the curtains were closed, leaving not so much as a sliver of space where I could get a glimpse inside my new house.

"Lucky we keep an eye on the place." The soft drawl coming from the woman standing on the walkway scared me half out of my skin and evoked the images of moss-draped trees and plantation verandas. I'd been too preoccupied to hear her coming.

"Otherwise, the copper plumbing might have been ripped out and turned in for scrap. Ever since the prices went up, there's been a run on break-ins of abandoned homes."

Heart still racing from being startled, I gave my soon-to-be neighbor a smile. "I'm Everly, and I just bought the place, so I can't tell you how much I appreciate your effort. Did you know Mrs. Willowby well?" Hopeful for any information I could glean, I joined her at the bottom of the steps.

Wavy hair the color of warm honey escaped the attempt to keep it pulled back and framed a face not much older than my own.

"Neena." The hand she held out carried smudges of paint around the nails. "Neena Montayne. I live right over there." She indicated the blue house across the street. "Welcome to town."

Suddenly my mother's odd reaction to my new address made more sense. As the cherry on top of my spectacular run of bad luck, it looked like I'd be living right on top of my ex-boyfriend and his wife.

If she let him back home, anyway.

"Thanks, but I'm actually a returning native. My folks live over on Maple, so I was born and raised half a mile from here."

Any hope of the same names being a coincidence died when she repeated mine. "Everly. It's Everly Dupree, right? I've heard of you." The chill creeping into her tone suggested what she'd heard hadn't been complimentary, and I suspected the welcome mat she'd laid out was in the process of being rolled up and stuck back behind the door.

What was I supposed to say now?

I went with dead honesty since I was too tired to think of anything else. "Look, I don't know what you've heard, but I've had a lousy few days, and I came home to relieve stress, not add more of it to my life."

Okay, maybe not full honesty since I didn't mention her husband had been knocking the headboard against the wall in the room next to mine the night before.

Neena gave me a serious blank face, so I added, "Or to yours."

If what Jacy had said about Hudson was true, Neena might not be in the exact same boat as me, but she sure was getting her oar tangled in the same lily pads. "I've sworn off men for life, and even if I wanted to hang my single shingle out, it wouldn't be pointed in Hudson's direction. All I want now is to find a job and to settle down in my new place."

Another assessing moment passed while Neena registered the fact that I knew who she was.

"Mrs. Willowby kept a clean house, and she made really good hoecakes." I took the return to our previous topic as a concession, but only a fraction of the stiffness left Neena's body, so I knew it was a small one. I nodded as if I had the slightest idea what she was talking about, and didn't try to stop her when she turned to leave.

"You should talk to Spencer Charles about a job. I heard he was looking for some help."

"Been there, done that." My mutter at Neena's retreating back went unheard. What was it with that man? Was he the only person in town looking to hire? If so, I was sunk.

Duprees don't sink, girl. They soar. Don't you dare let a run of bad luck clip your wings.

Having my grandmother's voice as my subconscious was kinda cool, and if I lived even half the life she had, I'd consider my days well spent when the last one came to a close.

What would she have done in my place?

Easy. She'd have gone back to Spencer's office with her new resume and set camp until he gave her another interview. Charm, guile, tact, she'd have used every weapon in her arsenal to get the job. Grammie Dupree had guts and spunk and a fiery spirit, while I felt like I'd been dunked in the swamp until my fire went out, then hung up to dry.

So many hits in rapid succession had me swinging like a pendulum over a pit of self-pity. Part of me wanted to stop moving and examine the pit, but the rest was afraid I'd fall in, and it looked deep. I thought if I stayed occupied and moving forward, I'd eventually get to the place where it all smoothed out again.

So long as I managed to find a job to go along with my new house, I'd call it a win.

And so, filled with misgivings, but channeling my grandmother's indomitable spirit, I pulled up in front of Spencer's office, swiped on some fresh lipstick for a confidence boost, and prepared for battle.

The front desk area was empty, but I heard Spencer talking on the phone, so I settled in to wait. The closed office door muffled the words, but his tone sounded impatient. Though, from what I'd seen of him, that was his brand of normal.

The phone call ended, and before I had a chance to knock, he yanked the door open. Seeing me there, his eyes widened, but that was the only hint I'd surprised him. "What can I do for you, Everly?"

"My resume." I handed him a single sheet. "With references." Charm and guile flew out the window because something about him just flat rubbed me wrong, but he needed help, and I needed a job, so I fought my desire to walk away and waited to see what he'd do.

"Okay." He gave the sheet a quick scan, turned back to drop it on his desk, then ushered me out and locked the door behind him. By the time I mustered up what I wanted to say, he was slamming the door on a shiny red two-door something or other that looked sleek and took off like a bullet.

Way to not get the job, I told myself as I slid behind the wheel of my current ride, the moving van of shame.

Half of me wished I'd taken my mother up on that dinner and the other half looked forward to burying her head under the covers for the night. Instead, ten minutes later, I found myself staring at the last two pieces of pepperoni pizza spinning around in the warming oven at the gas station near the motel.

Orange grease pooled between ropes of congealed cheese, the edges had started to curl up, and I had almost decided to go for an overpriced box of dry cereal when the door whooshed open to let in a guy carrying a stack of pizza boxes.

"S'cuse me." After setting the boxes down beside the warming oven, he reached past me to yank open the glass door and scoop up the dried-out slices.

"You're late, Ray," the man behind the counter-accused. "You missed the supper rush, and now I'll end up throwing half my profits in the trash."

"Get off my case, Bud." Red-faced, the pizza guy snarled. "I just went a round with the coach for pulling my boy outta the game." With sharp, nearly violent motions, he transferred the fragrant pizzas into the warming oven. "I'll give you a discount if it's such a big deal."

I stared after him as he slammed out the door.

"Don't mind Ray," the man said after the door had closed. "He's determined his kid deserves a full ride to Louisiana State on an athletic scholarship. Got a helluva pitching arm on him, but keeps getting in trouble with his grades."

"That's a shame," I said, for lack of anything better. "The pizza looks good, though." Because it was there, I went for the pepperoni and a slice covered in peppers, onions, and black olives. The veggie slice never made it out of the parking lot, and I debated going back for another, but common sense won out over hedonistic leanings, and I reluctantly backed out of the space and headed home.

The day was looking up, I thought until I turned the corner and saw Hudson limping toward the motel. My conscience wouldn't let me pass him by, so I pulled up alongside.

"Hey, you need a ride?"

His was a face I knew well, so when he looked up at me with hooded eyes, I knew I should have kept going. Hudson was in a mood.

"I'd heard you were back in town."

There was no graceful way to deal with the inevitable fallout of running into my former high school sweetheart. I'll be the first to admit I hadn't handled breaking up with him in the best way. Or at all, really. I'd returned his class ring along with a letter telling him I wanted to start college with a fresh slate.

Rumor had it he'd taken the split poorly, but what did I care? I'd moved on and would never have to be in the same room with him again. See, that's how you screw yourself over—by tempting fate with such stupid ideas.

"It's good to see you." My voice rose a little at the end, making it almost a question, and I searched his face for clues to his state of mind. Maybe the mood had nothing to do with me; he had moved on, after all, to marry the lovely Neena. We were probably fine after all these years, and something else was stuck in his craw.

"Did you leave your husband a note or did you dump him in person?" he growled, lip curled.

Or not.

If Jacy was right, Hudson had a life crisis going and didn't need me adding more weight to what he already carried. "I'm sorry, Hudson. Truly sorry. I could have handled things better at the time, and I chose to take the easy way out. You deserved more. Now, do you want that ride or not?"

For a moment, his spine went rigid and I thought he would throw the apology back in my face, then he relaxed and released a huge sigh. "Sure. Thanks, Ev."

Some of the clouds seemed to have lifted when he landed in the passenger's seat, but I saw his eyes flick toward the back and take in the jumble of my possessions.

We rode in silence for the two minutes it took to get to the Bide A Way.

"We're here," I announced unnecessarily and popped the door open before the engine died. I'd had enough awkward encounters for one day and wanted this one over as quickly as possible.

Hudson didn't seem to be in as much of a hurry. He followed me to the back of the van and watched while I surveyed the stack of boxes to see if I remembered where I'd packed my laptop.

"How did you find out where I was staying? I'm not buying that you ended up here by coincidence," he said, then his eyes slid down over me and back up to rest a few inches south of my face.

I'd been prepared to eat my pizza with a side of crow, but I drew the line at adding a canned worm appetizer, so I said nothing. He wouldn't believe me anyhow.

"We had some good times, didn't we?" With a familiar gesture, he reached out to tuck a strand of hair behind my ear. No matter what he'd done to get himself into trouble, he'd been sweet to me when we were dating, and I'd cared for him in the desperate way teenagers do, so I didn't want to hurt him now.

"We did." Hoping he'd get the hint, I turned my attention to shifting boxes to find the one I was looking for which was, of course, closer to the front of the van than I'd remembered. Just my luck.

"If I can't patch things up at home, maybe we could pick up where we left off. You know you were my first love."

Unfortunately, I couldn't return the sentiment, and this was not a conversation I wanted to have while I was on my hands and knees in the back of a moving van. My only option was to do the awkward reverse crawl which gave him a great shot of my backside.

Nothing he could say was enough to tempt me now. Especially not after meeting Neena. So, when he leaned in, I backed away and busied myself gathering my purse, laptop, and the rest of my dinner. "I'm sorry, but no."

Leaving him staring, I went inside and closed the door firmly behind me. Coming home had seemed like the only option when getting away from Paul was all I could think about. I could rebuild my life around people who loved and supported me. It would be easy to find a job and a place to live. The rose-colored view from behind my glasses hadn't accounted for the fact the world had turned while I was gone.

My appetite had flown, but because it was there, I nibbled on the lukewarm pizza while coming to the conclusion being popular in high school meant less than diddly squat in the adult world. You might be thinking I was a little old to be figuring out one of the basic tenets of life, and you'd be right. But better late than never, right?

In the fake twilight created by the motel drapes, I fell asleep long before the sun went down. Three eventful days in a row had taken their toll, and I slept like the dead until Hudson's banging headboard disturbed my slumber yet again.

What a jerk. How long did he wait after hitting on me before lining up another option? I rolled over and checked the bedside clock to find it was still early, so the answer was not very long. The first order of business the next morning, I decided, would be asking for a new room at the other end of the motel. I just wanted to sleep without having to cover my head with a pillow.

Was that too much to ask?

When I dropped off the second time, it was to muddle through a series of confusing dreams featuring Paul and Hudson as the same man, and both of them were speaking in angry tones.

I was almost glad when a muffled thud startled me awake.

Thick-tongued and bleary-headed, I couldn't tell if the noise had been real or a remnant from the crazy dream. Loath to go wandering around outside in the middle of the night, because who knew what might be lurking in the darkness, I listened until my heart stopped pounding. Other than the low growl of a car engine as it passed, I heard nothing out of place.

Somewhere in the middle of listening, I drifted off and didn't wake until the next morning.

CHAPTER 8

The long night of sleep and weird dreams unsettled me, so when I woke the next morning, the only way I knew to keep the raw emptiness from swallowing me whole was to avoid looking at it too deeply. *Stay active*, I cautioned myself. *Focus on the future.*

Easy to say, not so easy to do. Not when the future you're trying to focus on is a moving target.

To keep from wallowing, I made a list of the things I needed to do. Item one: move rooms.

On my way to the office, I noticed Hudson's door stood slightly ajar. With the way my luck had been running, he was probably spying on me.

Or not. The inside of the room was dark and quiet.

All the better. He'd had an active evening, so he'd probably sleep right through any noise I made during the transfer, but I would not be jolted out of another night's sleep. Truer words were never spoken. Or thought, as the case may be.

"Oh, Everly! I'm glad you stopped by. I forgot to give you this when you checked in." The motel clerk—I still couldn't remember her name and didn't want to admit that by asking her for it—opened a cabinet and handed me a travel-sized coffee maker. "Did I tell you about the mini-fridge? Every room has one built into the bedside table, and I always forget to tell our guests."

Since I'd not noticed anything that looked remotely like a mini-fridge, I suggested she might want to get some cards printed up and leave them in the rooms, and then I explained my reason for coming by.

"Do you think it would be possible for me to change rooms? I know it's an inconvenience, and I'll pay extra if there's a difference in price."

Now that I wasn't trying to remember it, her name popped up from the depths of my memory. Barbara Dexter looked at me with a hint of speculation but cheerfully altered the paperwork.

Then she handed me a new key and shamelessly fished for information. "I heard you bought the Willowby house, so I guess you won't be staying past the week."

I wondered by how many hours that news had beaten me back to the motel. "No. Unless it takes more than a few days for the paperwork to finalize, but Mrs. Tipton seemed to think everything would go through quickly." Probably to keep me from backing out of the deal. If I hadn't had such a good feeling about the place just from standing on the porch, I might be more concerned.

"House could stand some redecorating, but it has good bones. Catherine kept a nice place."

Why did people keep using the word bones when the house had a reputation for being haunted? Every time I heard that phrase, I pictured a house-shaped skeleton with a toothy, gaping grin. Not a comforting image.

"You knew her well? Mrs. Willowby, I mean. If you've actually been in the house, can you tell me what it's like in there? Is there anything I should be concerned about?"

"Sure I knew her, visited more times than I can count. Land sakes child, you don't believe all that haunted house nonsense, do you?"

"No, of course not." I mostly told the truth and then admitted, "I'm only curious what it's like. You see, there was a deadline on the bid, and I bought the place without…um…seeing the inside."

Left eyebrow shooting up toward her hairline, Barbara unsuccessfully hid her amusement. "You bought a pig in a poke."

I juggled the coffeemaker into the crook of my other arm. "I guess. What exactly is a poke?"

"Old word for a bag. Doesn't matter. Catherine would love to see someone young living in the house. Don't you trouble your pretty head, you're going to settle right in and make a cozy home for yourself."

I noticed she'd skirted the question of what the house was like, but I didn't want to press, so I took my new key and my tiny coffeemaker and headed back to my room to pack up my things. If I were lucky, this would be my next-to-last move of the week, and Hudson wouldn't do anything to make it more difficult.

His door was still open.

Something is wrong. The conviction whispered through my head.

Wrong. Wrong. Wrong. With each step closer to Hudson's door, the echo increased in volume until I had to look inside and see for myself.

Dazzled by the morning sun, my eyes couldn't adjust enough to catch a glimpse of anything inside Hudson's motel room, so I reached out to push the door open wider. It made a creaking sound that slid a shudder over my skin like water and raised the hairs on the back of my neck. Cold fire pooled in my stomach and turned my insides to jelly.

I smelled the coppery tang before I saw the blood pooled on the carpet under Hudson's tumbled body or his eyes, empty of life and staring. An ice bucket lay near his head, a smear of blood on the base.

It was just like the one I'd taken when it was offered the night I checked in—thick and solid-walled, with a hammered aluminum exterior that looked like it hadn't seen a lick of polish in years. The inside was still shiny—probably because it was coated in clear, hard plastic. Add the insulated metal lid, solid base, and sturdy handle, and even empty, the thing was heavy enough to make a solid weapon.

In mystery novels, the heroine always takes the sight of a dead body in stride, but I wasn't one of those. I screamed and out of reflex, threw the coffee maker. It flew up and over my head to land on the concrete behind me. The glass pot shattered, and I screamed some more. Long and loud until Mrs. Dexter ran out of the office.

"Call 9-1-1. Get help, I think … Oh, hurry, please. I think he's dead."

Surprisingly fast for a woman her age, Barbara ran back inside.

Air wheezed in and out of my lungs, but not enough to keep me from hyperventilating. The only coherent thought I can remember having was to stay outside, so I didn't contaminate the crime scene.

Hey, I watch TV. I know these things.

My legs trembled too violently to carry me very far, and I only just made it to one of the bright plastic patio chairs lining the area under the roofed-in overhang. Colors swam as a million bees buzzed in my head. On the brink of passing out, I remembered enough basic first aid to jam my head down between my knees.

Because the hum and buzz had eased, I heard Mrs. Dexter hurry past me, the whooshing intake of her breath when she stepped up to the doorway and looked inside. "Mercy sakes. Someone has killed the poor man." She sounded surprised.

"Didn't I just say he was dead?" Shock sharpened my tone.

Barbara didn't miss a beat. "You said dead, not murdered." Sighing, she seated herself next to me.

You haven't experienced surreal until you're sitting in a plastic deck chair arguing semantics over what to call a dead body with someone you barely know. The frustrating conversation pushed back the horror long enough for me to gather myself back together.

That lasted until I caught a glimpse of Hudson's legs through the fully open door and a wave of sorrow closed my throat. A siren wailed in the distance as my first tear fell. Yeah, Hudson hadn't seemed to let the separation from his wife affect his sex life, but he didn't deserve to be bashed over the head.

Fine gravel shot out from under his wheels as Ernie Polk whipped the black-and-white a little too quickly into the parking lot. When the cruiser door creaked open to disgorge his bulky frame, Ernie's face was a few shades paler than its normally ruddy hue.

Barbara rose to meet him, and to her credit, she didn't dither around. "Hudson Montayne's gone and got himself murdered," she said before he had a chance to open his mouth.

"Don't get too hasty," Ernie shouted over the noise of the approaching ambulance. "Just show me where he is and let someone with the proper training decide if there's been a murder."

Blue eyes snapping, Barbara clapped her hands on jean-covered hip. "Well, he didn't bash himself over the head, but by all means, go on in and see for yourself."

Her voice sounded loud muttering into the sudden silence left when the ambulance driver killed the siren. "Damn fool thinks I don't know a murdered body when I see one." The plastic chair nearly overbalanced when she threw herself down on it. "Poor Viola, losing her boy like that."

Despite the tartness of her manner with Ernie Polk, both sorrow and pity played through Barbara's tone. Viola Montayne hadn't liked me much, but she thought the sun rose and set on Hudson's say so, and this was going to just about kill her.

I couldn't tell if the shock was wearing off or getting worse because I felt sort of numb while Ernie went through the motions of declaring Hudson's death a crime. Barbara pressed her lips together, I assumed to restrain an *I told you so* when he came out with his face set in grave lines.

"Body temp and lividity indicate he was killed sometime after midnight, and there are defensive wounds, so there was almost certainly an altercation. Being right next door, you must have heard something." Ernie hit me with an intimidating, flat-eyed cop stare that I didn't know he had in his arsenal.

"No," I stammered. "Well, I did hear something, but it wasn't exactly a struggle to the death if you know what I mean." It seemed Ernie didn't get the hint because he waited for me to say it right out. "Look, it's none of my business who he sleeps ... slept with, but I can tell you they were rattling the bedsprings before the evening news came on." Heat prickled over my face along with a blush of color.

"You didn't hear anyone come in or leave?" Raising an eyebrow, Ernie insinuated I should have.

"I went to bed early, and I'm not that light of a sleeper. I probably wouldn't have heard a car pulling in." I blushed again and cursed my pale skin. "I didn't hear anything until the headboard knocking started up." I turned to Barbara and tried to soften the criticism. "The walls here are really thin. After that, I buried my head under the covers and went back to sleep."

"Interesting," he commented, "how you ended up staying in rooms right next to each other given your history. Cozy."

If looks could burn, Barbara would have gone up in flames. "Yes, I thought the same thing when I found out. You should know I was on my way back from requesting a different room when I discovered the ...him ... Hudson. And you should also know we spoke last night. For the first time in years."

Ernie perked up. "In his room or yours?"

"Neither." I recounted the events leading up to the conversation.

"Hmm." Ernie checked the parking lot and jotted down the fact the truck was missing. "His truck's not here, so that backs up your story of seeing him walking." His tone said he didn't know whether to believe the rest or not.

I gritted my teeth until they hurt and then relaxed my jaw. "I wasn't interested in him, or in being disturbed every night by whatever or whoever it was he was doing. I didn't come back home looking to start things up with Hudson again. Or with anyone. I'm sorry I can't be more helpful, but I didn't hear anything or see anyone suspicious."

Even though he seemed to take me at my word, Ernie cautioned me about leaving town. Like I had anywhere else to go. "Does that mean I'm a suspect?"

"Not at this time. Just stick around, okay, Everly?" If he meant to be reassuring, he wasn't.

I turned my head away and covered my mouth with my hand when the cart rolled past, but still caught a glimpse of the black bag with Hudson's body zipped securely inside. Having finally settled back into a normal rhythm, my heart rate kicked right back up into overdrive.

"I'm still changing rooms. I really don't want to stay in my old one after what happened next door."

Now that the questioning part was over, Ernie's face settled back into the friendly lines I remembered. "You're not in any danger, I don't think." Again, less than reassuring. "I'll beef up patrol of this area, though."

His attention turned to Barbara, and it appeared I had been dismissed for the moment.

A steady stream of traffic inched past the Bide A Way while I carried my boxed-up items to the van and moved it over in front of my new room. Word travels fast in small towns, and death was bound to bring out the looky-loos.

Only one car pulled in, and I recognized it right away. You don't see too many bubblegum-pink jeeps running around, but her dad had paid for the paint job for her graduation gift, and Jacy said she planned on driving it until the wheels fell off.

It was a running joke that she married a mechanic's son to keep her baby in one piece. Like all the best jokes, there might have been a thread of truth running through it, but Brian didn't seem to care as long as Jacy parked her jeep in his driveway every night.

CHAPTER 9

The Jeep had barely rocked to a stop, its bumper mere inches from my knees when Jacy flung open the door and confirmed the grapevine was alive and thriving.

Her eyes, deeply hazel and rounded, stood out against pale skin. "Is it true?"

"Depends on what you've heard. I'm assuming Carol Ann Wilmette's still on dispatch." If so, the chances were good that everyone in town already knew the details and then some. Carol Ann never met a piece of gossip she didn't pass along to her best friend Amelia, and Amelia never heard a piece of information she couldn't twist into something salacious.

Then again, what could possibly be worse than the truth in this situation?

"Everyone's saying Hudson's dead. It's all over town that someone up and killed him."

Since the ambulance carrying his body was just pulling out of the drive, I didn't see any sense in hiding the truth.

"It's true. Hudson is dead." Somehow, saying it right out like that made the whole thing more real. Either that or the adrenaline level in my system had dropped. Whichever it was, my knees started to wobble, and when I pushed my hair back with a shaking hand, Jacy noticed and slid an arm around me for support.

If possible, her face went a shade paler as I let everything spill out. "It was horrible. I'm the one who found him. There was so much blood. His head. His eyes. Looking at me. Empty." My breath whistled in and out as the tears came. "I think somebody hit him with the ice bucket."

I broke down, the sobs coming faster as Jacy patted me on the back.

"Honey you've had a terrible week, and it just keeps getting worse. Momma's going to want to come out and burn sage to cleanse your spirit or some such nonsense."

Mention of LuAnne Wade brought a watery half-smile. Jacy's mother claimed she carried the reincarnated soul of an ancient shaman and didn't do anything unless she ran it past her spirit guides first.

"If I thought sage would clear my run of bad luck, I'd let her do it. Heck, I'd dance naked under the full moon and wave feathers around if it stopped the weirdness. Ernie told me not to leave town. Jace, I think I'm a suspect."

The dirty look Jacy threw in Ernie's direction told me what she thought of that, and after giving me another pat on the shoulder, she led me over to the Jeep and settled me into the passenger's seat.

"Even if you can't leave town, there's nothing saying you have to stick around here all day. You sit tight while I fix everything. "

Out of the side mirror, I watched her advance on Ernie and launch into a conversation that I didn't need to hear to know she was giving him a piece of her mind. He tried to keep her from getting a look into Hudson's room, but I saw annoyance give way to sorrow when she did. Because of her inherent Jacy-ness, she softened and patted Ernie Polk on the arm. Even annoyed, Jacy couldn't help but be supportive, and as far as I knew, this was the first murder he'd ever had to investigate.

Our little town ran more toward death by old age or car accident.

Returning with a sober expression, she pointed to my open door. "This your room? You have your key?"

I shook my head and waved my hand to indicate that it was in the room, then sat there while she gathered up my phone and my purse and locked the door behind her.

"Look at the line of cars. It's going to take forever to get out of here." Jacy's presence had eased some of the heaviness from the past few days, but not enough. The need to move, to run far and fast from my thoughts, at least for a little while, was like a bubble of pressure in my chest.

With a wicked gleam in her eye, Jacy grinned at me. "That's what Jeeps are for. Buckle up, buttercup. We're taking the scenic route."

Hands flashing, Jacy steered the Jeep around the back side of the motel, skirted the trash receptacle, then gently nudged over the curb and drove into the field behind.

"I've always wanted to drive through a field of corn, but this is close enough." Tall grass whipped along the undercarriage with a shushing sound while Jacy found and drove through what had to be every furrow and divot in a four-acre span.

Her grin, considering the scene we'd just left, seemed less disrespectful of Hudson's loss than a way to reaffirm life and eased some of my overwhelming sense of doom and dread. She kept up an easy chatter until we finally came out onto the main road and instead of turning right toward town, turned left.

"It's okay, you can relax now." She grinned at me and then looked pointedly to where both my hands, white-knuckled, clutched the chicken handle on the dashboard. "You've lost your mojo, woman. I remember a time when you'd have been standing in the seat, holding onto the roll bar and whooping at the top of your lungs."

Jacy's observation touched a raw spot. "My life doesn't feel especially whoop-worthy at the moment."

When Jacy took one hand off the wheel to find mine and give it a squeeze, I had a vision of my bloody body stumbling away from the Jeep in smoking ruins. Good grief, she was right. How far had I fallen? Who was this mouse of a woman inhabiting my body?

"Then again, I bought Spooky Manor yesterday. Seems like that ought to earn me a few points on the mojo scale."

Dumbfounded, Jacy spun the wheel and pulled over to the side of the road. Twisting in her seat to face me, she said, "What did you just say to me?"

"Oh, pull your eyebrows back down before your face freezes like that and scares dogs and little kids. It was an impulse purchase … you know, near the register." Not that far off from the truth. "It was an excellent deal. Cheaper than first, last, and security. And I'm building equity." According to my mother, anyway.

"But Spooky Manor. I mean … what if it really is haunted?"

Considering my viewpoint on that particular subject had been waffling ever since I handed over the check, the only thing I could say was, "I don't believe in ghosts, and I got a good feeling when I went over and tried to get a look through the windows."

A pickup truck roared past, so close the wind rocked the Jeep. Nearly losing her side view mirror wasn't enough to sway Jacy's attention. "Let me get this straight. You bought a house, and not just any house, but one with a reputation for being haunted, without even getting a tour of the place first?"

The look on her face went from surprised to the sympathetic frown normally used around the very elderly who are no longer in full control of their mental faculties.

"When you put it like that, it sounds a little—"

"Stupid?" she supplied.

"Well, well. Tell me what you really think." My defenses went up. "I was going to say reckless. Daring. Bold, even." A spark of fire flared to life in my belly—the first one in days that hadn't been born from fury.

"I'm getting an entire house—one with good bones according to people who actually *have* been inside—for less than the cost of renting an apartment. The place is a steal, and even if it is haunted, the ghosts can't be worse company than my lying, cheating, soon-to-be ex-husband. Now, does that sound stupid to you?" There might have been more heat in my tone than I intended, but I'd had the worst week ever.

Jacy swung her door open and exited the vehicle. What on earth was she doing? Dumping me on the side of the road? That would put a cap on the crappy week.

To my great surprise, she let out a loud whoop and went into a butt-shaking dance. "She's back," Jacy sang out, gyrated a few more times, then came around to pull open my door. "Get out here and celebrate."

"I am not dancing around on the side of the road like a lunatic. It wouldn't be proper considering the events of the day." But I was smiling.

My refusal didn't seem to put a damper on Jacy's enthusiasm, but she did get back into the car. "Well, you're halfway back, anyway." She yanked the shifter, put the Jeep in gear, and sped off down the road talking a blue streak about how we'd fix the place up and make it cozy.

Sighing, I let her voice flow over me like a soothing balm to the soul. I'd missed this—her—more than I'd realized. Enough that I lost track of all the turns she'd made and didn't recognize the road.

“Um, where are we going?”

“You have been gone way too long if you’re lost in your own backyard. I’m taking you out for a day of peace, a chance to unwind. We could both use a break.” Wrapped up as I was in my own problems, I wasn’t so preoccupied I couldn’t hear the stress in her voice.

“Is something wrong?”

Before Jacy could say anything, my phone rang, and when I fished it out of my purse, my mother's name was on the caller ID.

"Bad news travels fast. I'd better answer, or she'll keep calling until I do." By the time I got done reassuring my mother that I was okay, we'd made several more turns, the last onto a road I knew well.

“Sorry about that. ” Thumbing the power button, I shut my phone off. “No more interruptions. Tell me what’s going on.”

“It’s nothing really.” Jacy’s hands clutched the steering wheel so tightly her knuckles showed the strain. “Nothing to worry about.” Except she *was* worried. Had she been hiding something this whole time? Only a jerk would have missed the signs.

“Spill,” I ordered.

“It’s nothing, really. We’re here, so we’ll have to talk about it later.” Jacy slowed until the tires barely crunched over the gravel road.

“Count on it.”

Through breaks in the trees, I caught glimpses of diamond sparkles rippling over Elbow Lake—so named for the v-shaped curve that, from an aerial view, looked like a bent elbow. Filing away the determination to dig an explanation out of Jacy at a more appropriate time, I inhaled and let the smell of the lake push everything else away.

CHAPTER 10

"This place. It's like magic." Jacy put my thought into words. "Every time I come to the lake, I feel like a kid again. You remember the night the bat got into the camp?" Her dimples showed when she smiled, the lines of worry smoothed over for the moment.

"How could I forget? The sight of your mother in her nightgown and bunny slippers … holding the dishpan over her head to keep the bat from getting in her hair with one hand, waving around Denny's butterfly net with the other. A moment that will forever be burned into my memory. Remember my dad trying to get up on water skis?"

"I do," she replied. "You know we have some video footage of him floating around. I'll have Denny burn you a copy. I've missed you, Ev. I mean, I'm really sorry your marriage didn't work out, but I'm going to be totally selfish and say I'm glad you're home. Sorry if that makes me a poor excuse for a human being, but there it is."

"I missed you, too."

I'll admit to going misty-eyed when we rounded the final turn, and the cabin came into view. "It looks exactly the same." Constancy—a concept I'd come to appreciate in the past few days. Well, that and fidelity, but for entirely different reasons.

Cedar shakes stained tree-bark brown, and a green metal roof made the cabin blend into its surroundings as if it had grown rather than been built among the pines. An early summer coating of rust-colored needles carpeted the path to the porch and felt both crunchy and soft under my bare feet. I didn't even remember toeing off my shoes before stepping out of the Jeep, the action was so automatic.

"I wish I had my suit. The water looks tempting." An hour before noon, and the thermometer had already climbed into the sweat zone. What surprised me more than the desire to dive under the ruffled surface was the hunger evoked by the scent of burning charcoal coming from two camps farther down along the shore. After the events of my morning, I hadn't been sure my appetite would ever return.

Jacy swung the latch open and hung the padlock back on its metal loop before looking me up and down. "You don't look like you've put on a single pound since high school, so you can probably still fit into that pink bikini you left there the night you and Hudson—" The grin fell off her face as she remembered the reason we'd come here. "Anyway, there are plenty of suits in the dresser. I'm sure we can find something to fit."

While Jacy opened up the windows to let in the fresh air, I took a look around.

If the outside of the camp looked the same, the interior had undergone more than a few changes. Wide plank flooring made from pine, sanded and stained a rich walnut color, replaced the scarred vinyl I remembered. More pine, only in a golden tone, lined formerly unfinished walls and ceilings in the main area and in both of the small bedrooms.

"Hey, there's a bathroom. That's new." It was housed in a closet-sized addition.

"The incinerating toilet. I tell you it's the best invention of the century. No more trips through the slug zone to get to the outhouse in the middle of the night." Those slugs had been Jacy's pet peeve about spending a good portion of the summer three miles outside the nearest power grid. "No plumbing required and it runs off propane."

"Are these the same bunks? They look different than I remember."

To accommodate the extra additions, like me, that Jacy or her brother Denny inevitably brought to camp, her father had nailed rough lumber horizontally to the studs on either side of the door and added plywood over the top of them to hold mattresses. Rough steps allowed access to the top bunks, and a privacy curtain made from old blankets ran down the middle of the room to separate the boy's side from the girl's.

"They're sort of the same." I heard cabinet doors opening. "Or mostly, anyway. You know dad never was good with his hands. I don't think he owns a level. When he had the walls insulated and finished, he asked the carpenter to use the old pieces and build something similar."

When I stepped back into the main room, Jacy stood in front of the open refrigerator door—it ran on propane as well.

"Lunch options are limited. We have condiments, canned tomato soup, and eggs. Probably should have stopped for supplies, but I wasn't thinking that clearly when we left. What do you think? Make do with what's here or drive back to town?"

It wasn't hard to read her tone—Jacy wanted to stay, and now that we were here, I did, too. "Soup and eggs work for me. Can't be worse than those peanut butter and pickle sandwiches Denny used to eat."

"He still does that when he comes up here, you know. Melanie says if she'd known he had such lousy culinary leanings, she might never have fallen for him." Jacy chuckled. "That's what he gets for marrying the head chef at a five-star restaurant. Still, she's at the point in the pregnancy where she's craving weird things, so maybe he'll get her to try one after all."

"This will be their second? Or is it third?"

"Second." Only because I'd known her for so long could I hear something off in Jacy's tone. "They had the ultrasound last week. It's a boy." She changed the subject back to food, and I let it go for the time being. "Do you remember where to find the herb patch? These eggs would taste better with some chives, and there's basil in the window box on the utility shed that should be far enough along to not miss a few leaves."

A pair of loons cruised into the mouth of the cove, ducked under, then resurfaced right in front of the camp, and I realized I'd never seen one loon alone. They always showed up in pairs. Pretty sad when birds are more constant than people.

My mood threatened to turn dark again, so I pulled my thoughts back from a pattern sure to turn into a spiral and collected Jacy's herbs. We ate our lunch sitting cross-legged on the dock and kept the conversation confined to memories of happier times. When the plates and bowls were clean, Jacy dug out bathing suits, including the infamous pink bikini—which only fit because I'd burned off some weight the past few days.

"Up for a paddle?" She tossed me a wrap that doubled as a towel. "It takes about an hour to get to the dam and back from here by kayak."

Ten minutes later, slathered in sunscreen, we launched from the grassy bank. It took maybe ten kayak lengths before my body fell back into the rhythm of dip and pull. Another five lengths before the rhythm emptied me out into a state of peace.

"Thanks for kidnapping me. I needed this." The light breeze had died with the coming of noon, its loss turning the water to mirrored glass. I was almost sorry when we reached the dam.

"*We* needed this." Jacy stopped paddling, let me pull alongside. "We've been trying for a baby for over a year. My doctor couldn't find anything wrong, so she referred us to a fertility clinic." Haunted eyes met mine. "We're going next week, but what if they say I can't ever have a baby? Ev, I'm so scared."

Turns out, you can't hug a person from one kayak to another without one or both of you tipping over, so I had to settle for an arm squeeze and verbal reassurance.

"We haven't told anyone yet. I didn't want to worry my folks, and Brian's mother keeps asking when we're going to give her a grandchild. I guess maybe I should have said something because talking about it makes it seem less overwhelming, but I didn't want to make them worry, too."

"I'm glad you told me," I said, holding an oar down in the water to keep the kayak from turning away from her. "There are so many alternatives these days, and it could be that you're just psyching yourself out."

Jacy sighed. "I know. That's what my OBGYN said, but we pushed for a second opinion because if a specialist says it's just nerves, I might be able to settle down and conceive. I think she was a little annoyed that we wanted a referral, but you know me. I'm a brooder."

"You're going to be a great mom, and I know it will happen for you. And if you need me for anything, I'm here."

Jacy inhaled a deep breath through her nose, then blew it out her mouth. I could almost see most of the tension leave her body. "Okay. Good. I'm good now. Wanna head back?"

We turned and paddled in companionable silence until we were within sight of the camp. I heard the loud, droning sound just before the bee went by the end of my nose with barely an inch to spare.

At least, I thought it was a bee because I caught a glimpse of yellow as the body flashed past.

"Whoa." I don't care who you are--when something that big with a stinger gets up close and personal, you freak out a little. I tried to maintain my dignity, and just paddle faster to get away from it, but the bee took my apparent lack of interest as a challenge, sped up, and buzzed my head again.

I ducked, and it circled back around. I ducked again and tried to paddle in a different direction. The bee landed on the front of the kayak, and while I didn't want to kill it, I also didn't want to get stung, so I dipped my paddle and sent a splash of water in that direction. Not enough to hurt it, but just enough to give the idea it should find a dry flower. You can't really aim water well with a paddle, so the bee escaped unscathed, but took off to buzz me a few more times, and eventually landed in my hair where I could feel its creepy feet scrabbling to hang on. I froze.

Meanwhile, Jacy had circled around and was waving her life jacket in my direction.

"Get it off me," I begged, but it took forever for her to get close enough to help.

The bee took off and, ducking every attempt to splash water on it, buzzed me several more times while I yelped and ducked and tried to get away, and while Jacy giggled.

Well, she giggled until the bee decided she was a better target and went after her. Then it was my turn to circle around and try to help. This went on for ten seconds longer than forever but was probably closer to five minutes—the bee dodging and buzzing us like it was on some kind of mission, while we circled each other, waving paddles and life jackets around.

Finally, the bee lost interest and flew away leaving behind a pair of disheveled women who immediately put paddle to water and got the heck out of there.

In the aftermath of the battle, I never noticed the figure standing on the camp's dock until I glanced up on my way toward the grassy knoll at the water's edge. "Ugh, what's *he* doing here?"

"Hey, David," she called as we bumped the bank. "I didn't know you were coming up here today." She added *be nice* to me in an undertone.

I know it was irrational to dislike the man for no good reason other than a childhood prank, but I couldn't help myself.

"I'm meeting your mom to go over the plans for the landscaping she wants to do. She should be along any minute. Might be a good idea if you two resolve your differences before she shows up."

I exchanged a confused look with Jacy.

"What are you talking about?" Since he was trying too hard to avoid looking at anything but my face, I assumed his imagination was taking him places I didn't want to hear about, so I peeled apart the hook and loop attachment and tugged the towel wrap up over my breasts, settling it snugly in place. "Have you been out in the sun too long?"

Everything about David made me annoyed. I wasn't sure why.

"Me? Look, ladies, I'll admit I found your little bout of kayak jousting more than entertaining."

When Jacy giggled, it hit me what he meant, and I supposed our bee encounter might have looked a little odd from a distance. We had, after all, been paddling serenely along before all hell broke loose, and from the dock, I doubted the bee was visible. Even if I could see the springboard he'd used to jump to conclusions, I didn't appreciate the meddling.

Jacy explained, through tears of laughter, that we'd been attacked and were merely attempting to protect ourselves. David appeared slightly disappointed that the story was tamer than the one he'd worked up in his imagination, but made no further comments. It was a good thing, too, because my patience with him was, inexplicably, wearing thin.

"So," Jacy said after she'd caught her breath, "my mother is on her way, then?" She directed the comment to David, who had evidently managed to insert himself into every corner of my life, from my relationship with my parents to my friendship with Jacy and her family.

It didn't occur to me at that moment that his intentions had nothing to do with me, but it still irked.

"I'm already here. Jacy, dear, I didn't know you were coming to camp today. I don't know how to say this, but I have some awful news about someone you know. Two people, in fact."

"It's okay, Mom. I already heard. Look who's here with me." Jacy stepped aside to reveal my presence.

Since I stood behind Jacy, I didn’t see whatever look she gave Momma Wade (the name Leandra insisted I use), but it got the job done.

“Everly, you’re a sight.” Moving around her daughter, Leandra kissed me soundly on both cheeks, then on the mouth before enclosing me in a patchouli cloud of a hug that went on for a beat longer than comfortable and ended when she shivered. “There’s something odd—”

CHAPTER 11

Pulling back, Momma Wade took my face between her hands and stared at the empty space near my left ear. When I tried to turn my head to see what she was looking at, she increased her grip to keep me in place. I couldn't see anything out of the corner of my eye that I thought would cause her to make tisking noises.

"What? Is something wrong?"

Jacy's face popped up over her mother's shoulder, and when she waggled her eyebrows at me, I knew this was one of *those* moments. The ones that had everything to do with spirit guides and prescriptions for anointing myself with oils and putting herbs under my pillow to ward off evil.

In other words, Momma Wade was about to get her hoodoo on.

"Jacy, can you get my bag out of the car? You know the one. I need to smudge Everly before the cloud over her gets any darker."

Oh man, it was worse than the oils, which I actually didn't mind since most of them smelled so good, but white sage made me cough. "It's okay, you don't have to—" Saying no to Momma Wade was as futile as trying to turn the wind. And don't tell anyone, but given the week I'd had so far, I kind of hoped a good smudging would change my luck even if it did cause me to hack up half a lung.

I almost didn't care that David watched the spectacle with amusement. If he hung around long enough, he'd get the smudge treatment eventually. Everyone did, and if this one worked, I might be around to give him the same amused face when it happened.

It didn't take but a minute for Jacy to bring the requested items, and Momma Wade lit the sage. Circling me and wafting the smoke over me with a feather, she cleansed my aura or whatever until I began to feel sick from the smoke.

"Mom, it's enough. I don't think this is helping." Jacy gently tried to pry the smoking bowl from her mother's hand. "Everly's turning green. Let it go."

Still focused on me, Leandra shrugged her daughter off. I'd never seen her that determined. "I need to … there's something … show me how." I assumed that last was an exhortation to her spirit guides and gave Jacy a frantic look. Another minute of inhaling the scent of burning sage and I might toss my cookies, or rather my eggs and soup, all over the place.

To my great relief, Momma Wade handed the smudge bowl off to Jacy, who dumped the smoldering herbs into the fire pit and suffocated them with a layer of heavy ash. The smell clung to my hair, but at least the air was clean when I sucked in a deep breath to clear away any lingering smoke from my lungs.

"Give me that." Leandra indicated the bowl, and I worried she was going to start all over with a new batch of sage, but she didn't. Instead, she told Jacy to hold the bowl while she muttered to thin air and searched through her bag of, well, I wasn't sure what all was in there.

Essential oils, for one thing, I learned when she popped the stopper off a blue bottle and shook a few drops into the ashes still clinging to the bottom of the bowl. Leandra was harmless, and even if I hated the scent of burning sage, I would never hurt her feelings, so I waited and watched as she pulled out more bottles and carefully added a drop or two from each.

When she was satisfied with the blend, she used her finger to stir the oils together with the powdery ashes until the mess turned into a dark gray paste.

"Don't be scared, Everly."

In case you were wondering, telling someone not to be scared has precisely the opposite effect, so I went from feeling indulgent to apprehensive in a hot second.

"What are you going to do?" Before I finished asking, she'd smeared the smoky-smelling oil across my forehead, and I went from feeling nervous to feeling foolish.

Whatever mania had come over her, Momma Wade was done with it now. Her shoulders relaxed, and the glazed look left her eyes. Her smile, when it appeared, looked totally normal. "There, your third eye is open. That should do the trick."

Dismissing me, she turned to David. “Come, young man, show me what you have planned for our little oasis by the lake.” Taking him by the arm, she led him into the camp.

“Well, that was—” Jacy stared at my forehead like she expected an actual eye to sprout there.

“Weird.” I finished. “Creepy. Intense.” My brain supplied a few more terms I couldn’t say out loud for fear of hurting Jacy’s feelings.

“All that, and by the way, you stink.”

“I hope you mean that literally and not figuratively.” But I followed her back to the dock and watched her dive neatly into the water. “Race you to the buoy and back.”

David was gone by the time we staggered back onto the porch, but Leandra was inside, putting away the last of our lunch dishes. Her face, when she turned toward us, revealed nothing of her earlier concern for my spiritual welfare.

“Now tell me, is the rumor true?”

How sad was it there were so many possibilities, I couldn't pick which one she meant? "Maybe. What have you heard?"

We settled in at the table.

“I heard you were the one who found poor Hudson this morning. Such a pity.”

Jacy chided her. “We came out here to give Everly a chance to get her bearings. Maybe she’s not ready to talk about it yet.”

"It's okay, Jace. I'm sure the gossip mill is running at high speed. I might as well hear what's going around so I can be prepared for the onslaught."

As gently as she could, Leandra began to roll out a laundry list of fact and supposition. “As you well know, he was staying at the Bide A Way, and depending on who’s telling the story, he left his wife because she took a lover or she kicked him out for the same reason.”

“Pfft.” Jacy hooted. “I wouldn’t blame her if she did. He could be a jerk sometimes. You heard the way he talked about Everly after she left. I wanted to kill him for it.” When she realized what she’d said, her face pinked. “I didn’t. Obviously. Why would I wait until now?”

Did I want to know what he’d said about me? Probably not.

"Then there's the incident at the school. A lot of speculation about why he was demoted, but no one's really certain. The only thing I know for sure is there was a closed-door meeting between him, the principal, and the superintendent when it happened. That came right from Sandy Dabond, and she works in the office, so you know that's prime information."

"Okay Mom, but you know people call her Sandy Dumb Blond, right? I'm not sure I'd take her word as gospel for anything." Jacy rose to snag a couple of bottles of water from the fridge. "What else have you got?"

Leandra twisted the top off her bottle and took a healthy swig. "Nothing else I want to repeat. Tell me, dear, did you really buy the Willowby place?"

I sighed. "Are you going to talk about the house's bones? Everyone does, and I'm hoping they mean it's solidly constructed, but I'd rather hear what it's like on the inside. No one wants to talk about that nearly as much."

"I'm afraid I can't help you there, dear. I've never set foot inside the place. I only brought it up because I think it takes an adventurous spirit to start over in such a decisive way. Don't pay any attention to what people say. Small towns are full of vipers who try to sting a strong person with words."

Reading into her tone, I came away with the impression that Momma Wade hadn't much cared for Mrs. Willowby who, by all accounts, was a nice person. Whatever the story was, she didn't seem to be in a mood to elaborate, and I'd had more than enough drama for one day to press the matter.

When Jacy made noises about getting home to start dinner, I was more than happy to help stow the kayaks away and close up the camp.

The trip back went by a lot faster than I expected, but when Jacy started to pull into the parking lot of the Bide A Way, I told her to keep driving. We'd been gone for a good six hours, but the place still buzzed with police activity. There was crime scene tape up running around the poles supporting the overhang and a satellite van with the Channel Five logo on the side.

"Are you sure you don't want to bunk on our sofa for the night?"

Tempting as it sounded, I wanted what passed for my own bed these days. “No, but if you wouldn’t mind running me back to the Gas N Go, I’ll grab a sandwich or some pizza, then maybe you could loop around and drop me off out behind the motel. The way the false front on the office sticks out, I think I can sneak around the corner and into my room without being seen.”

“I’ll go you one better.” The steering radius on the Jeep was tight enough to pull a U-turn almost on a dime, and Jacy did so with such flair I had to grab the chicken handle again. Two minutes later, she nudged into a narrow space near the back door of the diner. “Stay here, I’ll be right back.”

She couldn't have been gone five minutes before she was back with a bag of take-out containers. "Mabel's the best. I told her the gist of things, and she bagged up Bert Thompson's order. He'll have to wait a few extra minutes for his meatloaf tonight."

“Thanks, Jace. Tell Mabel I’ll settle up with her tomorrow. It ought to be safe to show my face without being mobbed by then.”

“I’m working breakfast in the morning; it’s my short shift of the week, so I get off early. Offer still stands, you call if you need me.”

Only a criminal would sneak into her own room when she hadn’t done anything wrong, but since the alternative was being interviewed on the news, I sucked it up and waited until the coast was clear. The U-haul van blocked me from sight, and I was glad I’d moved it during all the hoopla. Besides, I couldn’t have stayed in that room. Not after what had happened right next door.

CHAPTER 12

Determined not to relive the memory, I turned my focus to the take-out bag and the scent of Mabel's meatloaf. Enjoying, or at least attempting to enjoy, a meal took nothing away from the dead, and I told myself I needed the sense of normalcy.

That eating what amounted to a stolen meal in a cheap motel room had become my new normal was not a topic I wanted to explore right then. Or maybe ever. Better to just put one foot in front of the other until I was back on solid ground.

Glancing over to where I'd tossed my purse on the bed, I noticed the corner of my phone sticking out. Half tempted to leave it off and just go to bed, I sighed, tapped the power switch, and listened to the wake-up tone. According to the number on the little icon, there were seven missed calls and several voice mails.

Two of the missed calls came from the town office, two more were from my mother, one from Spencer Charles, and the others from numbers I didn't recognize.

Dialing up my voice mailbox, I put the phone on speaker.

Everly, darling, please call me. I know you said you were okay, but I need you to check in. Mom sounded worried.

Miss Dupree, this is Martha Tipton from the town office. I'm calling with good news. I rounded things up early, and we managed to talk the title company into pushing the paperwork through. I'm pleased to say you can come in and pick up a copy of the paperwork and the key to your new home anytime tomorrow. Well, not any time, since we're only open from nine until noon on Fridays.

That was the best news I'd had all week.

Spencer Charles here. I've checked your references, and if you are still interested in the job, it's yours. Call me as soon as possible to verify, but as far as I'm concerned, you can start on Monday.

Even better news. The kind that lightened my mood considerably.

For about a minute, and then the next message played.

Everly Dupree, I know you had something to do with my boy being killed. You should have never come back to town. You're going to pay for this. Do you hear me?

I hadn't heard that voice in over five years, but even through the huskiness brought on by grief-stricken tears, I recognized it as belonging to Hudson's mother.

The next few were from reporters, and I deleted them without listening to any of them all the way through.

Mom answered on the first ring. "Everly, I'm so glad you called. Are you all right? Let me send daddy over to get you. I don't think you should be alone right now. It's not safe there."

"It's okay. I'm fine." Well, as fine as a person could be in such a situation. "And it's only for a night or two. I'm picking up the paperwork and keys for the house tomorrow, and once I get the utilities switched over, I'll be moving in. That's good news, right?"

Reluctantly, she let me distract her. "It's very good news. I have the day off tomorrow. Would you like me to go with you to look the place over?"

"I'd love that. I'm planning on getting the keys at nine. Do you want to meet me there, or should I pick you up?"

I heard the smile in her voice and realized she had probably expected me to say no. "I'll meet you there. Now, I hate to be the bearer of more bad news, but there's something you should know."

I switched the phone to my other ear. "About the house? Don't tell me you've changed your mind about it being a good investment."

There was a pause, and my heart began to sink toward my toes.

"No, of course not. It's about the unfortunate incident this morning."

Unfortunate incident? A man was dead, I'd classify that with the use of stronger language. Tragic would be a lot closer to the truth.

"Hudson's mother has been telling everyone who will listen that you're the reason her son is dead."

"That's not news to me. She got my number from someone and left me a nasty message. I'm choosing to give her the benefit of the doubt because she's lost her son and she's hurting. No one could possibly believe I had anything to do with his death. I hadn't exchanged more than a few words with the man in years. Hudson's part of my distant past. What reason would I have to kill him now? His mother's delusional."

When my mother gets flustered, she fiddles with her hair. I could picture her doing that now.

"I just thought you ought to know what's being said."

"Because her Fruit Loops don't float and now she has people believing her?"

"One or two, maybe."

I really didn't know what to do with that information, though. Take out an ad in the paper saying I hadn't killed anyone? Had people forgotten they ever knew me in the short time I'd been gone? I'd grown up with a good reputation in this town. I had been the homecoming queen, for crying out loud. How did I go from that to being some sort of murdering Jezebel?

"I'll be careful. Don't worry about me. You'll see me tomorrow, and then you'll know I'm really okay."

Mollified, she let me off the phone, so I could settle in with my thoughts and try to sort out the yo-yo effect my life had taken lately.

"That wasn't a very nice thing to say about my mother. Come on, Ev, give a guy a break."

When Hudson's voice came out of the empty space two feet behind me, several things happened all at once. My knee slammed against the underside of the table when I nearly jumped out of my own skin, my heart tried to crawl up my throat while my stomach headed south, and I couldn't decide if I needed to scream or pee.

Hey, if you've never seen or heard a ghost, don't judge my response. And if you have, then you already know what I was feeling. I don't remember moving, but I ended up with my back against the door, staring at the nothing where I thought I'd heard him speak. My brain told my fingers to turn the knob and open the door, but the message didn't get through.

Have you ever had one of those dreams where you know the boogieman is right behind you, baring his jagged, ugly teeth, but you can't move? Every cell of your body is screaming run, and you are paralyzed.

Yeah, that can happen in real life, too.

“Okay. Everly, you’re okay.” My voice sounded louder than it should, and I didn’t even feel weird that I was talking to myself. “It was just your imagination. Breathe.” Which is good advice if you’re not so steeped in adrenaline breathing goes from a basic bodily function to a chore. It was humiliating to realize I probably wasn’t ever going to be the best person to have around in a crisis.

“Yeah, go ahead and breathe. That’ll help.”

This time I did shriek. Just a little. Because this time, I could see the faint, hazy outline of Hudson, like I was looking at him through a shower door.

“You can’t be here.” The paralysis lifted enough for me to point a shaking finger at him. “You’re dead.”

“No kidding. I hadn’t noticed. Thanks for stating the obvious.”

With a nauseating waver, my vision of him began to clear. Oddly enough, the look on his face—equal parts frustration and fear—calmed me down.

“I don’t … I can’t … this is …”

He shot me a grin. "Do that for another hour, and you might catch up to me."

The burning question of the day popped out. “Why me?” Okay, the burning question of the week, or the new theme of my life. I hoped not, because seeing ghosts on top of everything else? Not cool. “Why?”

“You’re the only one who can see me.”

Of course, I was. Why wouldn't I be? Because wasn't that just the toy surprise at the bottom of the box? A flare of hot fury burned off the rest of the adrenaline, and I advanced on him as if getting all up in his face would do any good.

“Get out of my room. In fact, get out of my life.” I don’t know why I thought it would work, but I aimed forked fingers at him.

Hudson only laughed. “Come on, Ev. I’m not the devil.”

Next, I tried waving my grandmother’s cross necklace in his face.

“Or a vampire. Geez, Everly. What is your damage?”

As a last ditch effort, I grabbed the last of the salt packets Jacy had thoughtfully included with my meal, ripped off the top, and with a flourish, sprinkled it in his general direction.

He tossed me a raised eyebrow, which, when I think back, was an indication of how far off the rails I’d gone.

“Are you done?” Hudson sort of hovered himself into a prone position on my bed and crossed his arms behind his head. “I’m not leaving until you agree to help me, so you might as well calm down.”

Never, in the history of ever, has telling someone to calm down resulted in the desired effect. This time was no exception. Sending a glowering look his way, I picked up my phone and typed in: what gets rid of ghosts? Just my luck, the first thing on the list was smudging the area with sage.

“It won’t work. You can try it, but I’m not leaving. I’ll just wait outside and follow you everywhere.” He’d left the bed to look over my shoulder. As threats went, his was fairly effective because I couldn’t stop him without surrounding myself in a perpetual haze of sage fog, and I wasn’t doing that.

“Please, Ev. I need your help.”

Sighing, I gave in to the inevitable. A new pattern in my life. “If I help you, you’ll go away afterward? I mean, you’ll like … I don’t know … move on or rest in peace or whatever?”

“I hope so, but if you help me figure out who killed me, I’ll leave you alone even if I'm stuck like this forever. Deal?" He held out a hand, and like an idiot, I reached out to seal the bargain. Instead of warm flesh, I thrust my fingers into shivery cold.

I shuddered. “Deal, but don’t touch me again. Or it’s off. You hear me?” Bargaining with the ghost of my dead high school boyfriend. Yeah, that’s totally normal—if the word has lost all meaning.

“If we’re doing this, let’s get it done fast. Tell me who killed you and I’ll pass the news along to Ernie Polk.”

Hudson ran ghostly fingers through ghostly hair. "If it was that easy, don't you think I'd have opened with that information? The last thing I remember is you giving me the brush off, and then everything went fuzzy. Next thing I know, there's a bunch of people wearing disposable jumpsuits swarming all over my room, and talking about how I was dead, and examining the evidence. None of them could see me. A little while later, you came home, and there was something about you," he squinted at my forehead. "That made me think you would be the person who could help. The rest you know."

I considered his explanation, but none of the information cleared anything up. By then, my heart rate was heading back toward normal, and the only thing left from the adrenaline rush was a nasty case of dry mouth.

A ghost. Could I really be talking to a ghost, or as my mind insisted, a figment of my imagination? I settled back in my chair and contemplated my half-eaten dinner until the silence pressed down so hard I had to speak.

"If you can't remember who killed you, then you must at least have some idea why. Who had a motive for wanting you dead?"

He took longer to answer than I thought he should have. I mean, how could he not know who his enemies were?

"I can't." Panic settled over his face. "Something's blocking my memory." He opened his mouth and tried again to get the words out, and when he couldn't, panic turned to anger. Face red, eyes squinched tight, Hudson's soul or essence or ghostly form—I'm not sure of the correct term—began to vibrate so fast I had trouble focusing on him.

Tension built in the room until my ears popped with it and it felt like my eyes might as well. The comforter and pillows flew off the bed to land in a heap across the room, and the pressure that had built suddenly collapsed.

Like lousy reception on a cell phone, Hudson faded in and out, become less substantial with each passing moment until he went transparent and then was gone.

Great. Now I'd spend the rest of the night wondering when or if he would show back up. When he did, if he did, we were going to have to talk about establishing some rules.

When my alarm went off at eight the next morning, I dragged myself out of bed after a mostly sleepless night. I'd have given much to have been awakened in the night by Hudson banging on the headboard rather than imagining him hovering over my bed. And here I'd been worried about buying a haunted house.

"Hudson! Are you here? I'm going to take a shower. No peeking. I'm warning you." I justified talking to what might or might not be an empty room, because I needed the shower without him skulking around. Or idiocy had set in.

It was the fastest shower on record, mostly spent craning my neck around to make sure I was utterly alone. Yeah, we were going to have that talk when he showed up. Boundaries. I needed boundaries.

When I pulled back the curtains and looked out, the parking lot appeared empty of police cars or news vans, but I grabbed my purse, phone, and car keys and made a mad dash just in case. I wanted to leave myself plenty of time to settle up with Mabel for the takeout from the night before, grab a cup of coffee, call Spencer to accept the job, and get to the town office right when they opened.

This was shaping up to be another busy day.

Even though it was Friday, I hoped I could convince the power company to come out and turn on the lights. Otherwise, I wouldn't be able to do much until Monday, and since I'd be starting work then, I'd have only the evening to unpack and return the moving van.

On the plus side, Mrs. Tipton had said the house came with everything in it so I might be able to put a bedroom together. Or maybe that would turn out to be on the minus side. Who knew? With the way my luck was going, I wasn't sure if I should be excited or apprehensive, so I allowed for a little bit of both.

CHAPTER 13

Still bleary-eyed, I missed seeing the news van parked in the side lot at Mabel's, which was why I was shocked when Jacy intercepted me at the door and dragged me around the corner and out of sight.

"What did you do that for?"

"Where'd you park?" Her head swiveled as she searched the lot, and her eyes were wide and frantic.

I pointed a thumb over my right shoulder. "Over by the back entrance to the power and water office. Why?"

"Okay, good." She blew the stray hairs off her forehead. "The news team is just finishing up their breakfast in the diner, and they've been asking practically everyone about you. I knew you were coming in this morning, so I've been watching for you. I've got to go back in, but Mabel said to tell you to go around to the kitchen entrance. She'll let you in through the back." I finally got a grin from her. "If her rep wasn't on the line, I think she'd have spit in their eggs."

Half tempted to go in and confront the news team just to get it over with, I thought of the house key and Mrs. Tipton, and decided skulking around wasn't a sign of weakness—just the prudent thing to do at the moment.

"No worries. First, I'll go see if I can sweet talk the good folks at power and water into sending out that handsome husband of yours to turn the water on today. They're open now, right?"

Technically, Jacy's husband Brian only worked for the water district, but since the power company maintained a local presence in the same office, I figured he might be able to wield some influence there, too. With power and water, I could borrow dad's tent and camp out in the backyard of my new place if necessary.

"Yeah, it's after eight." Satisfied she'd saved me from being featured on the five o'clock news, Jacy headed back inside but tossed a suggestion over her shoulder. "You ought to make a detour into Foss's for a floppy hat and sunglasses."

It took all of five minutes to do the paperwork. Having Mrs. Tipton call the power company office to verify the transfer of ownership was only a formality since everyone in town knew I'd bought the house. The next five minutes I spent listening to speculation about recent events and securing Brian's promise to hook me up first thing. He was on the phone pulling in a favor when I left.

The news van was gone by the time I crossed the street and pushed my way through the diner's front door.

"You know I love you, but girl, you look like something left over from a cat fight." Mabel ran my debit card through the reader, and at my request, added a breakfast sandwich and coffee to the total from the night before.

"Thanks, it's good to know my outsides are running on par with my insides."

"You want that to go?" Jacy asked, then followed up with, "You could have called me if you were having a rough night. Isn't that what friends are for?"

No one would believe the true story, so it was easier to let her think my pride kept me from taking her up on the offer of a place to stay.

Still, Jacy took offense. "Being stubborn is not one of your finer traits."

"But I'm so good at it. I've elevated it to an art form." Lame comeback, but I'd had a rough night.

With swift, annoyed movements, Jacy poured coffee into a to-go cup and slid the sandwich into a bag. "Yeah, you're the Picasso of pigheadedness, all right."

"Don't be mad, Jace. It wasn't for the reason you're thinking." She wouldn't believe me if I told her why I'd spent a sleepless night, so I distracted her with other news. "In a surprising twist of fate, I got the job at the mortgage place. Oh, and I'm picking up the keys to the new house today. I don't suppose you'd want to come help me make it habitable."

Her mildly annoyed expression smoothed out to something more cheerful. “Okay, I’m off shift at eleven, and I can do laundry anytime. I’ll be over as soon as I clock out. I can’t believe I’m finally going to get a look inside Spooky Manor.”

"What do you say we stop using that name for it now that I'll be living there alone?" Not that I was scared of the place anymore. It's funny how personally being haunted changes your perspective on the concept, but if it were all the same to Jacy, I'd rather my house not get a reputation for being ghost central. At least not any more than it already did.

To soften the critical blow, I shot her a smile that I hoped hid my nerves. It was too late to turn back now. All I could do was hope I’d made the right choice. “Wish me luck.”

Stuffed with bacon and eggs on the lightest, fluffiest biscuit I’d ever tasted, the sandwich gave my stomach something else to do besides being the runway for a flight of butterflies. By the time I pulled in at the town office, the clock said 9:07, and I felt halfway human again.

“Everly,” Mrs. Tipton greeted me warmly. “I have your paperwork right here. This is your deed, and this is the bill of sale. You’ll see where I’ve indicated the back taxes are paid and you’ve put a deposit on the taxes for the upcoming year. I’ll send you a letter come the first of September to let you know the actual amount. There might be a balance owing or maybe even a credit due. I won’t have the numbers until the final assessment.”

Fifteen rent-free months would free up money to make a few updates. It seemed as if home ownership should come with more pomp and circumstance than a slim sheaf of papers in a folder. The whole process seemed a bit anti-climactic. Maybe it would all feel more official when I turned the key in the lock.

“I saw the power truck turning down Lilac on my way here, and I already spoke to Brian Dean, so you should be all set to go.”

That she didn’t bring up Hudson’s untimely death took me by surprise. Probably hooked into the grapevine at the root level, and didn’t need to pump me for details, I figured.

“Thanks, Mrs. Tipton. I can’t tell you how much I appreciate this.”

I couldn’t tell if she wasn’t on the receiving end of thank you often enough, but I caught a fleeting expression on Mrs. Tipton’s face that struck me as out of place, but I took the proffered folder and the wad of keys she dangled in the other hand. The bundle weighed heavy. How many rooms did this place have, anyway? At a glance, I saw six or seven skeleton keys and at least that many newer, flat ones.

"It's a good house."

"So my mother says." I shot Mrs. Tipton a grin. "She's going to meet me there. Thanks again."

My luck was turning around. Finally.

CHAPTER 14

I was so excited I barely remember the drive between the town office and my new home. My mind raced with wondering how many rooms, and what did the kitchen look like? What possessions had poor Mrs. Willowby left behind? Most importantly, would I be able to move out of the motel right away?

Somewhere under all the more immediate issues, there was the thought that Hudson's ghost—if it was even real, and at this point, I was still trying to talk myself into thinking it wasn't—might stay tethered to the area around where he'd died. Moving out of the motel might get him off my back altogether. One more check in the plus column.

My mom rose from sitting on the top step when I eased past the electric truck at the end of the driveway. From the look on her face, I knew I wasn't the only one struggling with experiencing moments of pure happiness in the face of tragedy.

She pulled me into her arms when I came around the corner of the van. "I'm so sorry you have had such a rough time of it these past few days, but I'm happy you're home." Her arms tightened, and I held on, too.

"This is a new start for me, even if it's been a rocky launch." I kept an arm around her waist as we stepped up onto the porch. "I'm scared to open the door."

"Then it's best to do it fast, like ripping off a bandage."

Good advice, though impossible to take because I had to sort through a handful of keys to find the right one.

"It will be the last one you try," Mom said.

"Always is." A running joke in our family.

After five tries, I found the one that fit. With my heart in my mouth, I twisted it in the lock just as the lights flared inside. The timing of the power coming on was either perfect or creepy.

The first thing I saw was a set of stairs leading up. Dark. Oak or maybe walnut, I couldn't tell for certain under a year's worth of dust, but the balusters were well and ornately turned. Cleaned and polished, I thought the warm tones of the wood would gleam. Striped wallpaper in muted rose tones against a yellowed background made the entrance a little darker than my preference but was in good enough shape that I wouldn't have to do anything with it right away.

So far, so good.

Closed doors hid the rooms on either side of the entrance.

"If I remember correctly, that's the front parlor." My mom pointed to the door on the right. I have no idea what that one leads to," she rattled the handle of the door on the left. "In these old houses, most of the rooms are small but plentiful. The kitchen is down the hall. The kitchen is down the hall on the left, and there's a less formal living room directly across. There's a half bath between that and what used to be the dining room. When Catherine couldn't handle the stairs, she had it remodeled into a bedroom. Those are the only rooms I've seen, but the house goes on a ways because of the addition on the back."

Then she surprised me by jumping up and down. "The joists are solid. There's maybe a little sagging here and there, but that's just settling due to age. Farmhouses in this era were built from whatever came to hand. Rough lumber, peeled posts and beams. But the ones like this, built for the wealthier families, were more refined. You can tell by the trim work and," she ran a hand over the wall, "the smoother quality of the plaster."

"Is that what everybody meant when they said the place had good bones?" I didn't want to tell her I had no idea what a joist might be.

She nodded and headed toward the kitchen, so I followed her past a line of photos I assumed were of the former owner.

Taking one down, I called out. "Mom, wait. Is this her? Mrs. Willowby, I mean." I spun the frame so she could see the apple-cheeked beauty gazing up at a handsome man. She wore a white dress with short sleeves and a lace overlay and didn't look a day over sixteen, but I thought this must be her wedding photo. Mr. Willowby cut a fine figure in his pleated pants under a matching jacket with V-shaped lapels and a slight nip in at the waist. A fedora shaded one side of his face but did nothing to hide twinkling eyes, and a fond smile. They looked happy. I sighed at the reminder of wedding-day bliss.

Mine had been much the same. Too bad it hadn't lasted.

Mom turned, looked, and nodded. "Beautiful, wasn't she?"

I had to agree. How sad for this happy young woman to end up dying alone. Maybe Mrs. Tipton was wrong, and there was still a family somewhere. If so, I hoped they'd forgive me for being the erstwhile heir to her history.

"She was." I walked down the hall, watching Catherine Willowby and her husband age from one photo to the next. Toward the end, she looked to be in her sixties, dressed in wide-legged slacks and a polyester blazer in the last photo on the wall. "No kids?"

Mom had joined me. "Sadly, no. They were never blessed."

Still holding the wedding photo, I asked, "Why don't I remember her? You clearly were close enough friends to have visited her here, and Mrs. Dexter talked about attending parties in this house, so how did I never meet Mrs. Willowby?"

The reply came after a moment of musing followed by a sigh. "Basil passed when you were six or seven, and I think he took a large part of Catherine with him when he went. She stopped throwing parties and became something of a recluse after that. You would have enjoyed her, much as she would have found you delightful. Catherine loved children, and since she could never have her own, tended to dote on any she managed to spend time with."

I thought of Jacy. "That's really sad." And now I felt like a jerk for fostering the reputation of this house and walking wide around it when I was young. Had I known the true spirit that resided here, I might have made a friend.

I'm sorry, Mrs. Willowby, I'll take good care of your place, I promise. If I'd been alone, I would have spoken the vow out loud.

Standing in the hallway, looking at her smiling face, I knew that if Mrs. Willowby did indeed haunt her house, I would welcome her presence as she would welcome mine. I'd been silly to worry. This was not a spooky place.

The revelation left me feeling all warm and fuzzy inside. I should have known that much sentiment would come back to bite me on the butt.

Hanging the picture back where it had been, and with a light heart, I made my way toward the kitchen.

"It's a little cluttered, and the wallpaper is busy."

"And you're the queen of understatement. In fact, there's your crown." Or crowns, anyway. A stack of the paper ones from Burger King took up space on the top shelf of a corner cabinet. Busy was a kind word for the wallpaper. Over an off-white background were three versions of pink-and-blue berry-filled baskets. Each basket was backed by green leaves and framed in brown and tan filigree, and they all marched in diagonally repeated patterns that made my eyes want to cross.

My snarky comment earned me a raised eyebrow. “But if you look past that, you’ll see the cabinets are of good quality and design.”

Taking her word for it, I squinted and imagined the cabinets set against a solid color. Maybe a sunny yellow or, for a more contemporary look, a pale gray. Paul would have preferred the gray, my mind insisted on pointing out. Then yellow it was. Or better yet, a saucy red. Anything but gray.

While I made that decision, my mom continued. “The appliances are dusty, but appear serviceable.” She switched on one of the stove burners, but nothing happened. “Did you call to have propane hooked up?”

Oops, a detail I’d missed. “No, I’ll do that today, though.”

She pulled out her phone. “I’ll make the call. I know the owner quite well, and I can get him to send someone over right away.”

Taking my cues from her and ignoring the decor, I tried to see the assets for what they were. The dishwasher looked new, and the refrigerator was definitely not of the same vintage as the range since it had ice and water in the door. It slid out from the walls on wheels so I could reach the electric plug, and came right on with a satisfying hum.

“I’ll check—” A knock interrupted before my mom could finish her sentence. “That’s probably David.”

I had to clamp down to keep from whining. “David? Did you ask him to come over?”

“No, I didn’t. Daddy wanted to come to check out the furnace and get the water heater going, but he has another week of classes and then workshop week. Anyway, when David heard your father fretting about not being able to come and help, he volunteered."

While she offered no reproach, I realized she assumed David was the reason I hadn't spent any time with them since my abrupt return to town. "That's what decent men do."

It was a dig at Paul, and for once, I agreed with her.

Because I made no move to do so, she started down the hall to let David in.

When he bent down to give her a kiss on the cheek, my blood pressure shot up to the red line. How dare he be that nice to my mother? Yeah, I knew how petty that sounded, and I didn't care. He might not be carrying a frog, but I still didn't trust him, and everything he did seemed designed to make my mother like him more.

"Hey, Everly. Nice place. It's a good thing you found out about it before I did, or I'd have snatched this baby right up. Look at those moldings, and the baseboards are pristine. You got a gem here."

They were all lovely sentiments, and probably genuine, but all I heard was that he planned to stick around town if he could find a place.

There was a pause while my mother's gaze tried to bore a hole through me, and then I forced myself to thank him for coming and make idle chitchat. He'd come over to help, and my mother hadn't raised me to be churlish.

"Where's the basement?" His gaze flicked toward me, but he addressed the question to my mother.

Mom shrugged. "You know, we hadn't explored enough to get that far yet. We were checking out the kitchen first."

"Old houses like this usually have over/under staircases."

Whatever that meant.

As long legs carried him down the hall, he added over his shoulder, "Saves space." He disappeared around the corner behind the stairs toward where my mom had indicated there was a living room.

"Bingo!" drifted out of the short hallway created by the rear of the stairs. "It's locked, though. You got the key?"

Mom grinned at me conspiratorially. "We've got keys. Lots of keys."

I went back to the kitchen and retrieved them from where I'd set them down earlier. The bundle made a heavy handful, and when I dropped it in David's hand, he whistled and looked up at me.

"Which one?"

"Well, it's not that one. I pointed to the one that had opened the front door. Otherwise, your guess is as good as mine. It's going to take me half a day to try them all and make labels."

Twisting the bundle in his hand, he contemplated them as if they were a puzzle he needed to figure out.

"That one there and the one next to it look like car keys. Do you mind?" Not waiting for an answer, he unlatched the hook and began easing keys off the ring. "It's not this one, or this, or this." Looking for a place to put them, he strode into the kitchen and began to sort the keys into piles on the table.

The two he'd designated as car keys went into one pile. The key I'd shown him earlier he set off to one side. The rest, as he sorted, looked a lot the same to me, so I had to ask. "What's the difference between these and those?" I indicated two piles that to my eye looked quite similar.

"These are solid, those have a pinhole shank." Flipping them up, he showed me the hole at the end of the key. "The basement door takes a hollow-shank key, so it could be one of these. They all have different bit widths and lengths. This one's notched, that one isn't. Then you have some that are the modern, flat type. Those are newer, more secure."

"You sure know a lot about keys." I didn't mean to sound suspicious, but I think I did anyway.

"My first job was with a locksmith. Fascinating work. Anyhow, these are the possible matches for that door. It's your place, so I'll let you do the honors. There's something about turning the keys in your own locks for the first time. It's like magic."

I wouldn't have gone so far as to call it magic. If I'd had access to magic, I'd have turned back time and listened to my mother when she told me not to drop out of college and marry Paul.

Without commenting further, I took his choice of keys and headed back to try them in the door behind the stairs.

CHAPTER 15

The second key worked, and the door creaked open with a blast of chilled air up from below. I shivered, but this was my house. I was going down those stairs if it killed me.

David gently nudged me aside and felt around for the light switch.

"I'll see if I can find a flashlight."

"No need," he said and pulled a penlight out of his pocket. The meager spear of light barely pushed back the dark. "There." Pointing the beam for me to see, he traced the path made by a string tied to the pull chain of a bare bulb fixture and run through a series of eye hooks to dangle next to the door frame. "Cheaper than installing a switch, I suppose."

I followed him down the stairs. About halfway to the basement floor, we hit a small landing where another string hung near the railing post. That one turned on another much brighter bulb, and I got a glimpse of a narrow, brick-paved floor. The air was cool but dry, which was a good sign.

As if he couldn't help himself, David gave his opinion as he roamed through the space. "Foundation looks solid. No leaks or signs of water damage. Might be worth paying for a home inspector to take a look around, but I'm not seeing any major red flags so far."

Reassuring as it was, I just wanted him out of my house so I could see the rest of the rooms.

"Furnace is newer, and a brand known for being efficient and trouble free."

"I'm glad it gets your stamp of approval." That time I managed to bite back the sarcasm. "Sounds like you know a bit about furnaces, too. Your second job?" I even threw him a grin, and it didn't hurt my face.

Which he returned. "Third, actually. Though I guess it wasn't technically a job. I built houses with Habitat for Humanity for three summers in a row. In fact, I hitched my way south and had the honor of working on one with Jimmy Carter."

Good grief, next he was going to tell me he'd given away a kidney. As if I didn't already feel like a loser for having mean thoughts about him just because he was sleeping in my old bedroom while I was camped out at the motel. Didn't stop them from coming up, though. Even a saint could feel like a rock in your shoe under the right circumstances, I guessed.

With as little sleep as I'd had the night before, his energy tired me out, but I was thankful he'd come. I'd never have figured out any of this by myself.

"Now to see if she heats up. We'll look for the furnace switch while we turn the power to the heater on at the breaker box. I'll just follow the wires leading from it and see if I can figure out where to look, okay?"

Saying no didn't seem like it would work, so I waved a hand to indicate he should do whatever he wanted to do and sank down on the landing to watch. He looked, he poked around, he tested the poles that ran from paving stones to the ceiling at strategic intervals. After five minutes or so, he finally decided he'd seen enough.

I didn't want to go up the stairs ahead of him because they were steep enough to put my backside at face level, but since the reverse held even less appeal, I didn't see any other choice. He probably wasn't looking anyway.

"Propane's here," Mom practically sang out when David closed the basement door behind him.

"What did you do to get someone so fast?" Being tired makes me snarky.

But my mom gave it right back to me. "I promised him sexual favors, of course."

"As long as they're not from me, I don't even care, and your secret's safe with me. I won't tell Daddy, but you'll probably have to bribe David for his silence. "

David held up both hands as if to distance himself from the conversation. Based on looks, most women would think seriously about making the offer, but even if he filled out a pair of jeans in all the hot ways a man could, he wasn't ever going to be my type.

With a twinkle in her eye, Mom answered the knock on the door and let the propane delivery guy in to test the stove. He couldn't have been more than eighteen, and I wondered if he'd heard our banter because the tips of his ears looked like they were on fire.

Keith, according to his name tag, said, "You're all hooked up. I'll just check the stove if that's okay."

I waggled my brows at my mom and led him to the kitchen.

When Keith left, I had a working stove and a bill for a little over a hundred dollars. Totally worth it. Meanwhile, David had found the breaker box and the furnace switch, so I followed him back downstairs because I wanted to watch. It turned out the furnace needed to be bled which involved a tube, a container, a wrench, and some really smelly oil.

"Listen, I know I haven't been the nicest person to you since I came home, but I do appreciate everything you're doing to help." I waved a hand to indicate the furnace and water heater. "Can I pay you for your time?"

To me, it sounded like a reasonable question, but I guess to him it came off as the ultimate insult.

"No. Thank you, but no." He pinned me with a look that made me squirm. "One of these days, we'll have a talk about how I came to be staying with your parents. Today is not that day."

"I'm sorry." The taste of crow wasn't nearly as bad as that of my foot in my mouth. "I didn't mean to … there's no excuse. I'll look forward to that discussion, but in the meantime, please accept my apology."

Sure I was tired, and yeah, my nerves were taut as piano strings, but neither of those things was his fault. He didn't respond, and afraid I'd make it worse, I turned coward, clapped my trap shut, and headed upstairs.

"Everything okay, dear?" Mom had her radar going.

"Fine," I lied. "It's a little overwhelming, but in a good way."

While I'd been preoccupied, my mom had found the key to the room she called a front parlor.

"It's dusty," I said when she all but dragged me in for a look. "But there are some nice pieces in here. It might be the perfect place to set up my library."

While the drapes were too fussy and I might not care for Catherine's choices in wallpaper patterns, the mix of antiques and newer furniture made my heart go pitter-pat. Nice pieces, not too ornate, and upholstered in subdued fabrics that I could totally live with. I practically heard my wallet sigh with relief.

Friction with David notwithstanding, this was turning out to be a good day.

Speaking of the man, he popped his head around the corner, scanned the wall, and retreated.

"Something wrong?" I called after him.

"I need to find the thermostat."

We found it in what my mother called the formal living room, and I abandoned the two of them to deal with things while I retrieved the rest of the keys and toured the first floor of my new home. My home. Mine. Mind-boggling concept.

I'd known the place was big, but I hadn't expected to find so many rooms. I could have lived quite comfortably in the downstairs section of the original structure alone. Then there was the upstairs and the addition on the back. Why on earth had Catherine Willowby needed so much space?

The doorbell rang, a lovely chiming sound, while I pictured the paint colors for the closet-sized bathroom in the remodeled bedroom mom had told me about—a charming room with access to the porch facing the backyard.

"Hey, Ev. Let me in. I come bearing gifts," Jacy called through the door. "Come on, I'm dying to see the place."

When I opened the door, the mouthwatering aroma of Mabel's fried chicken followed her inside. "I figured you guys might be hungry by now, so I grabbed lunch."

"Smells amazing. Want to eat first or take the tour?"

There wasn't time for Jacy to answer because the furnace fan kicked on before she could. I heard my mother's muffled exclamation—a word she normally never used—and saw a cloud of dust rise out of the heating vent in the hallway.

Uh oh.

Jacy and I hit the porch, and my mother and David weren't far behind.

"We should have cleaned the vents before we turned on the furnace." Mom brushed at her sleeve.

"Um, I guess it's a good thing I brought lunch. We'll eat while the dust settles." Jacy looked for a good place to sit, and since the porch was bare, set the bags down and settled in with her back against the wall. "There's chicken and coleslaw. I'm glad I grabbed to-go packs so we have forks."

She looked at David, who didn't seem certain whether the invitation extended to him. "Hey, before you sit down here, would you mind grabbing the cooler out of the back of my Jeep? I brought a bunch of soft drinks. Cleaning is thirsty work." Just that easily, she put his mind at ease. The magic of Jacy.

While we ate, talk inevitably turned to the tragedy of recent events. "Hudson's wife lives right across the street," Jacy pointed toward the house. "I wouldn't be a bit surprised if she went back home once he's laid to rest."

"I know. I met her the day I bought this place. I stopped in to look around, and she thought I was casing the joint, so she came over to warn me off. I feel bad for her." On so many levels. "She seemed nice, but she wasn't shy about checking out why I was here."

David finished first and pushed to his feet, whether to get away from the gossip or because he had other things to do, he didn't say. It wasn't like anyone was stopping him from leaving, but after my less-than-stellar behavior so far, I kept that comment to myself.

Flashing him a smile that would melt chocolate, Jacy said to him, "Would you be a dear and grab the vacuum cleaner from my front seat?" She dusted off her behind, then gathered up the empty food containers, stuffed them back in one of the bags, and put the empty cans in the other. "I brought a few cleaning supplies with me just in case. I know you said you'd take the weekend to settle in, but I'm offering my services to help things along."

I'd known Jacy since we were in diapers, and cleaning wasn't one of her favorite things to do. Unless she'd undergone a massive personal transformation in the past few years, she was angling for something.

"Tess called me right after I saw you this morning and asked if she could switch shifts with me, so I'm off until Sunday, which worked out fine since Brian's leaving this afternoon to go fishing with his dad for the weekend. I've got some free time—"

There it was.

“And you’re offering to help me clean so we can have a girl’s night in Spooky Manor.”

“Didn’t you say we weren’t supposed to call it that anymore? But yeah, if you’re planning on staying, I thought I might keep you company. What do you say, Ev? Are you up for a sleepover? Just for tonight, or maybe tomorrow night, too.”

I nodded, relieved she’d asked. “I guess we’d better get rid of a few layers of dust if we’re going to be spending the night here. Thanks, Jace, for making things easier.”

Staying alone in the house didn’t bother me, but just in case the whole thing hadn’t been a hallucination, I didn’t think Hudson’s ghost would show up if I had company. With that in mind, I had no problem with buying a night or two of peace.

CHAPTER 16

The early afternoon passed in a flurry of activity and the constant whine of the vacuum. When my mother discovered the little rotary attachment for upholstery, she practically yanked the machine away from Jacy and went to town. Woe betide the speck of dust that got past her, and she made sure I knew what she wanted for Christmas. The woman was in love.

I figured David would take off once we got started, and I was right. Except he wasn't gone long and when he returned, I heard a lawn mower fire up. That's another man thing, I think. The absolute conviction that knee-high grass must be tamed with a sharp blade. That he'd decided to mow shirtless was just icing on the cake. Not that I was interested, but he did make a pretty enough picture that Jacy sighed.

"Hey, you're a married woman."

"It's like a museum," she retorted. "You can visit and look at the art, but you don't have to take it home."

On that note, I changed the subject.

"Since you're staying, would you mind helping me unload the van and then follow me over to drop it off? It's not due back until Monday, but the closest drop off point is a garage that closes for the weekend, and I start my new job on Monday. I'm not sure what my hours are going to be like, so I'd rather just get it over with today."

I was going to miss having my own wheels but was tired of driving around in a freaking billboard that announced *Here's Everly, her marriage is over, and she's moving home again.* The news was out, obviously, but I didn't need to keep flying the banner.

"What are you going to do for transportation?" Jacy asked. "It's not like we're overrun with Uber or Lyft drivers around here. You want me to keep an ear out for a deal? People come into the diner, they talk."

"That would be great."

I'd barely flipped open the van's rear doors before David killed the mower motor and nudged us out of the way. "I'll get this. You just tell me where you want them." Normally, I'd have argued, but I'd already annoyed him once and he seemed determined.

A moment dragged by while I considered. I hadn't even seen all the rooms yet. "The front parlor. I think there's room for all of it in there. I can unpack once I've sorted myself out a little more. Except for the wardrobe boxes. Those can go in that far bedroom for now."

By three, other than the insides of one set of kitchen cabinets and running the drapes through the fluff cycle of the dryer to get the last of the dust out of them, we had the main downstairs rooms in decent shape.

"It's a lot of house for one person," Jacy said, her gaze traveling around the room. "Much more than you really need. I feel bad for that poor old lady, having to keep up with it. She must have been lonely."

While I agreed with Jacy's sentiment, it surprised me to realize I didn't feel overwhelmed. The welcoming feeling I'd experienced on the porch during my first visit had only increased since coming inside. I would be happy here. Alone or otherwise.

"It would make a great B&B if the upstairs has decent plumbing. A place like this could turn a tidy profit. The Bide A Way might be deserted right now, but we're in that lull just before school lets out for the summer. You wait another week or two, and the place will be packed. Ever since they started that revitalization project up in Hackinaw, we've seen an increase in tourist traffic and revenue."

All of that was news to me.

"I guess I haven't kept up on current events as much as I should. But Jace, doesn't that beg the question of why someone from town hadn't already bought this place? I mean, Mrs. Tipton said something about the house having to go through probate, and I think she mentioned something about the title process finishing early, but if this place has that kind of income potential, don't you think it's a little odd no one else was standing in line ahead of me?"

Jacy put her dust cloth down on the table and laid her hands on my shoulders. "Do you believe in fate? Because I do. If you were meant for this house, then don't you think fate would take matters into its own hands and put you on the right track?"

There was an opening for telling her about Hudson's ghostly visit. I didn't take it, though. I did consider pointing out her resemblance to her mother at that moment.

Before I could formulate an answer, she continued, "I'm sorry your husband turned out to be a no-good cheating jerk. Really, I am. But I'm not sorry you're back. I've missed you, and if you want to make this place into something, I'm here to help. If you want to rattle around here by yourself, I'm down with that, too. Fate brought you back, and now you'll figure out what to do. I have faith."

Picking up the cloth again, she went back to cleaning.

Right now, I couldn't conceive of anything I wanted less than to run a B&B, but there might be other possibilities to consider.

"Van's empty." David interrupted my thoughts. "I'm taking off. The lawn will need another pass in a day or two. I'll come back and take care of it."

"You don't have to—" I started to protest. He'd been nothing but helpful, and all I had done was act like a jerk. "I'm sorry. I haven't been very nice to you, and there's no excuse. My parents trust you, and that should count for something." I gave him a smile and tried to figure out why, every time my mother looked at him, I felt ridiculously jealous.

"I'll be back in a couple of days," he said, holding up a hand. "Really, I don't mind. Maybe then we'll have time for that talk." Turning on his heel, he stalked out of the kitchen. I yelled a thank you toward his retreating back, heard him call out a goodbye to my mother, and then he was gone.

I took a deep breath and made a note to apologize again when I saw him. It wasn't his fault I'd had a crappy week, or that I could see a spark in my mother's eye every time we were in a room together.

Besides, I really wanted to hear how such a capable man had ended up renting a single bedroom at my parents' house.

"He's cute, but there's obviously something going on with him," Jacy said, echoing my thoughts. "You ready to go?"

I nodded; she wasn't wrong. "Let me just tell Mom we're leaving."

I followed the sound of singing and found my mother wiping down the last windowsill in the living room. There was a streak of dust across the front of her jeans, and I picked a cobweb out of her hair. Come to think of it, I probably didn't look much better.

"I didn't think we were going to end up spending the whole day cleaning," I said. "That wasn't why I asked you to come over, you know."

The smile she gave me was so bright it would have lit up a cavern.

"You've come home. That's worth a day of cleaning. A week or two, even. Now, while you're gone, if you'll give it to me, I'll go collect your things from the motel and return the key to Barb. It's probably better if I'm the one to go in case there are still reporters hanging around. I can go and be back before your father gets home from work."

We'd made it through an entire day together with barely a harsh note. That was progress for us.

"Thank you. I was dreading having to go back there. And thank you for today." A wealth of emotion from everything that had happened in the span of a few days came over me all at once, and my chest hitched as I pulled her into a hug. She returned the embrace fiercely, and I thought I saw the shine of tears in her eyes when I turned away.

Yeah, things would be different between us this time.

"I love you, Mom. I probably haven't said that enough."

I might have said more, but the honking of Jacy's horn reminded me I had an errand to run.

After dropping the van, we hit the grocery store so I could stock up on the necessities. For Jacy that meant a container of cookie dough ice cream. A perfect choice, she said, since it combined two of her favorite snacks in one. Logic like that was hard to argue, and I was looking forward to an evening of girl talk and ice cream—we'd certainly burned off enough calories to eat as much as we wanted—and spending the first night in my new home.

I drew more than my share of curious looks as we made our way up and down the aisles, but no one approached me. That should have made me suspicious, but I was grateful. Not that I could blame anyone. I mean, what were people supposed to say? Welcome home, sorry you got dumped, and by the way, what about that dead body you found?

Yeah, there are times when being a pariah of sorts is just what the doctor ordered.

At the checkout, I kept my head down and didn't notice the donation can until Jacy pointed it out.

"Isn't that the saddest thing?" Reaching past me, she jammed some ones into the hole cut out of the coffee can lid. "Sixteen and diagnosed with cancer. That's Bobby Madison. He's Mabel's sister's neighbor's boy."

"He's who?"

"Mabel's sister's neighbor's boy," she repeated as if knowing such an odd set of statistics was nothing unusual.

Fishing through my purse, I pulled out some bills and picked up the can to add my contribution to hers. "This says they think they caught it in time, but he still has to have brain surgery. I feel bad for his parents—they must be a mess right now."

My heart went out to the bright-eyed, smiling teen on the can. He was wearing a baseball uniform and leaning against a beat-up sedan that looked vaguely familiar for some reason.

"The donations are to cover expenses so his parents, Patty and Daryll, can go to Boston and stay while he has the surgery next week." Apparently, my willingness to chip in had bought some goodwill from the checkout clerk who looked familiar in that way that people do when they've had five years to grow up while you weren't around. I couldn't put a name to the face, but since she'd offered me a smile to go along with the explanation, I gave her one in return.

Back a the house, my mother pulled in just behind us with my things from the motel. There wasn't much, so it took very little time to unpack the groceries and get everything inside. Still, she spent an extra minute or two watering and trying to find the exact right spot for the poor little plant I'd basically ignored for most of the week.

"Do you want to take it home with you?" I'd rather not have to look at the reminder of a job I'd enjoyed if I was honest. "Consider it a gift." Then I felt bad because she seemed so pleased and I'd been thinking only of myself with the offer. At some point, and sooner rather than later, I needed to get hold of my swinging emotions.

Once she was satisfied the plant would survive the few minutes it would take to get home, Mom went to put it back in the box.

"Oh, there was some other stuff in here." Along with my name plaque and the rest of the small things I'd used to personalize my desk, she pulled out a large mailing envelope. Everything ended up on the kitchen counter, and I forgot all about it while we followed her out to the car to say goodbye.

"We'll be over tomorrow to help a bit more. I'm warning you, though, your father will probably be up with the sun. I'll hold him off for as long as I can, but I'm not making any promises."

That I had more in common with my dad than my mom had always been one of the problems with our relationship, but we did share a baffled response to his cheerful morning nature.

Once she'd gone, Jacy and I rambled through the clean rooms and settled in the kitchen to put together a simple meal.

Halfway through the cooking, I realized I'd been opening cabinets and drawers and pulling out pans and utensils without thinking, I said, "Is it weird that everything in here is right where I'd have put it anyway?"

Jacy shrugged it off. "Great minds think alike."

"Maybe. It's still weird."

We spent the rest of the evening catching up on local gossip while avoiding the topics of marriage, divorce, or sudden death. No ghosts showed up to disturb our sleep, and for that, I was grateful.

CHAPTER 17

My parents showed up at a respectable 8:30 the next morning, and dad talked a blue streak about the trim and something called the soffit as he paced back and forth in front of the house. I didn't understand half the terms, but it seemed as if he thought mine were all in good shape.

After the downstairs tour was over, he asked, "Where's the key to the garage?"

"I'm not sure which one it is, but probably one of those." I pointed to the pile of flat keys David had set aside.

"Well then." He scooped up the lot. "Let's go find out." A kid in a candy shop was what he looked like.

"You go on ahead, dear. Jacy can help me with the bedroom." Because they were there, my mother had taken it upon herself to unpack my wardrobe boxes by swapping Mrs. Willowby's clothes with mine. For that alone, she'd be getting that vacuum cleaner for Christmas.

Moving into a fully furnished house might be a boon to my pocketbook, but living among someone else's things was mildly weird. Going through an old lady's underwear drawer felt all kinds of wrong.

Outside, my father examined the garage door lock.

"It's a Schlage," he announced as if that meant something important, and picked the right key on the first try.

Windowless, the garage was as dark as night inside, and I hung back while dad found the light switch. I say that like it was a concession to his manly need to investigate, but it was for purely selfish reasons. You can't see spiderwebs in dark rooms.

"The old lady was a fanatic."

I half jumped out of my skin and bit back a scream when Hudson's voice sounded right next to my ear.

Two deep breaths quieted my pulse except for the area that throbbed near my temple. So much for Hudson being a figment of my imagination, or for him not being able to find me once I'd moved.

"Well, would you look at that!" With Hudson nattering in my ear, I barely heard my dad's exclamation, but what was I supposed to do? I couldn't tell a ghost to shut up or give him a poke with my elbow. All I could do was try to ignore the disembodied spirit.

The *That* Dad was referring to turned out to be a whale of a car.

Reverently, my father ran a hand over the fender, his eyes gleaming with car lust. "This is a 1979 Buick Regal. Two-door coupe."

That was what he said, but all I heard was blah blah blah, old-lady car. It was maroon, two-tone with a lighter red roof, but I supposed it could have been worse, given I had no transportation at all. I made agreeing noises.

"I thought she sold it when she stopped driving." He paused to think. "Must have been ten years before she passed. It's a classic."

Hudson snorted in obvious disagreement. "It's a tank. She used to pay me to back this boat out of the garage, wash it, and drive her to the gas station to fill it up once a month. Picky, too, the old bat. It had to be spotless, or she'd short me on the money. Too bad she's gone, though. I could have used that money these last few months."

Since it was all I could do, I shot him a disgusted look. "It's a lot of car."

"It's yours now, right? You bought the house and the contents, so if it runs, you've got yourself a car." Dad cut to the heart of the situation. "A classic car." There was reverence in his voice.

"Look at that interior." Dad tested the driver's door and looked crestfallen when it didn't open. "It's locked."

"In this house, if it had a key, she locked it," I said, turning to go back inside. "Wait here. I know where the keys are. Let me get them." As I'd hoped he would, Hudson ignored the order to wait.

"You have got to stop popping up like that. You know I can't talk to you with other people around," I hissed at him on my way back inside.

"Well, I had to do something to get your attention. Why are you fooling around here? You should be out there trying to find my killer."

"I have a life, you know." As I heard myself say it, I realized the statement was incredibly insensitive. "What do you want me to do? The police are investigating, and I'm the last person you should be asking for help. I can barely keep up with my own problems at the moment. What makes you think I can deal with yours? Why don't you go haunt someone else?"

As he floated along beside me, his tone turned snotty. "The high and mighty Everly Dupree thinks I *chose* her out of all the people in the world."

I gave him a sideways look. "Who are you talking to? Are there other ghosts here?"

"You," he said, rolling his eyes. "But you're the only person who can hear me, so I guess you're either going to help me or I'll just stick around and haunt you for the rest of your life."

As threats went, I supposed his was a credible one. "Fine," I snapped, scowling. "I'll help. But you need to leave me alone right now. Come back when I'm not surrounded by people, and we'll talk. There are going to be rules, Hudson. And you're going to follow them, or I'll find a way to tune you out, and you'll be stuck here forever. Or maybe I can find a priest and exorcize you, or whatever it is they do to get rid of unwanted spirits. This is a two-way street."

I knew my threat was as hollow as a blown out eggshell at Easter, but it was all I had.

"You promise you'll help?" he said, floating along beside me.

"I said I would." Not that I had the first clue what to do for him. "But not now. Give me a day or two to settle in here, and then we'll talk."

As I went through the door, he faded away, but not without leaving a new load of doubt and worry behind. How was I supposed to find a killer? And if I didn't, would I end up stuck with him for the rest of my life?

CHAPTER 18

Pushing my worries to the back of my mind, I handed the car keys to my dad and watched him flit off to his happy place. Having a project—any project, whether working with wood, repairing something, or setting up his curriculum for the school year—put my dad exactly where he functioned best. At the heart of him, he was a problem solver.

While I was gone, he opened up the garage door to let in more light, and when I came back, I found him lying on the floor inspecting the undercarriage.

"Here are the keys," I said, and he popped back up to take them from me.

"She's clean, Ev. Not a speck of rust anywhere. The underside looks like it did when it rolled off the assembly line."

There's this odd thing that happens when my dad gets excited. His hair goes all...poofy. It's a weird, physiological response and probably where the term hair-raising comes from. In his case, it happens whether he's happy or scared.

When he's happy, like he was at that moment, the poofy hair flopping over delighted eyes, along with his broad smile, made my heart melt. I forgot all about Hudson and my ghost problem and let my dad's excitement infect me.

"That's great, dad." A car this old, even if it were in excellent condition, probably wouldn't get me much on a trade-in, but maybe I could drive it for the rest of the summer and save up some money.

Unlocking the door, he glanced back at me, and said, "Battery's probably shot, and it might not even run unless she came out and started it every so often."

I couldn't tell him she'd paid Hudson to take care of it once a week. "Maybe she did. I wouldn't be surprised. From what I've seen so far, Catherine Willowby was a meticulous woman." The more I'd seen of her house, the stronger the niggling doubt over why the town would let such a gem go for next to no money became. The numbers didn't add up.

"Fingers crossed." He popped the hood. "Battery's disconnected."

We spent a couple of minutes tracking down a wrench. His fingers made short work of tightening the connection, and he crowed when the single bulb mounted on the underside of the hood flared to life. "Looks like she's got some juice."

Then he went to muttering about fluids and levels, and something about the possibility of varnish in the gas tank. He pulled out a couple of dipsticks and then checked underneath the car a second time. "The floor is immaculate. No sign of a leak anywhere. Jump in and pump the gas once to set the choke, then let off and turn the key."

I did as he instructed and the engine flared to life.

"Listen to that. She's purring like a kitten after all this time. They don't make them like this anymore, Ev. She's a beauty." Jumping in the passenger's seat, he instructed, "Take her for a spin around the block."

"I can't, Dad. It's not registered, and the inspection ran out months ago." The way my luck had been running, I'd get a ticket before I made it to the end of the block.

"You'll be fine. The police have bigger things to think about right now than someone taking an old car for a test spin. Go ahead now, let's see how she handles."

We cruised—and believe me, cruise is the appropriate term for driving a land yacht—through town, took a right to cross the river, and made the loop back toward the Bide A Way.

"Turn left here. Take her down the lake road where we can open her up a little. Blow some of the cobwebs out of the motor."

I don't mind admitting I enjoyed the speed when I crammed on the gas and the old car wound up to seventy in no time.

"Feels smooth," Dad said, excitement laced through his voice, "and did you see she's only got thirty-six thousand miles on her? I bet she's worth close to five figures in this condition. You really scored."

There it was again. The notion that poor old Mrs. Willowby's death had been to my benefit. I pulled off on an unused road to turn around and slid the shifter into park.

I frowned and glanced over at dad. "Don't you think it's weird how this all happened? I mean, nobody buys a house this cheap and not only is the house in great shape, but there's also a vintage car worth far more than I paid, all by itself? It feels criminal to get so much for so little. Then there's the timing. It just happened to be available right when I walked into the town office. I'm beginning to think there's something wrong like it's going to turn into a money pit, or it really is haunted, and Mrs. Tipton railroaded me into taking it off the town's hands."

With all the swinging back and forth I'd done on the topic, my head was starting to spin.

When confronted with a dilemma, dad always went into thinking mode, and this time was no different. There was a long pause before he asked to trade places with me, and he still didn't speak until we were back in town.

"Look around." He slowed to a crawl and directed my attention down one after another of the short side streets. "How many *for sale* signs do you see?"

More than I'd bothered to notice before. "Quite a few. Why is that? Jacy said things were picking up around here because of the revitalization project up at Hackinaw."

The tour over, we turned back down Lilac Street. "Tourism is great for certain types of businesses, but it doesn't do much to shore up the underlying infrastructure of a town like ours. Sure, we've seen some growth in local commerce, but without a corresponding increase in the business sector, we don't have enough jobs to grow our tax base."

"So, why aren't people opening more shops to attract tourists?" Seemed like an easy solution to me.

He backed the car into the garage and twisted the key to kill the engine, but didn't make a move to exit the vehicle. "I expect some will, but in the meantime, we have a dwindling population and an increasing number of tax foreclosures on the books."

Understanding washed over me, followed by a tremendous sense of relief. "That makes more sense, then. Mrs. Tipton wasn't trying to railroad me—she was playing both sides against the middle by getting me a place to live so I'd become a tax-paying citizen and take a dud property off the town's hands. Doesn't explain away the car and all the furniture, though."

At that, Dad shot me his famous grin. "That was plain laziness. Catherine Willowby passed her final days in hospice care, so the house had already been closed up before it went back to the town. I'd put money on the fact no one ever bothered to check what was in here when they picked up the keys from the nursing home."

"So you're telling me I scored big on the deal because nobody bothered to take ten minutes to check the place out?" My grin matched his.

"It's a good day when everyone wins." Holding out his hand, he dropped the keys in my palm and his gaze gentled. "Are you okay? You've had a rough week."

I lifted a shoulder and nodded, blowing out an exhausted breath. "It feels more like a month. Daddy, do you know anything about why Hudson got into trouble at work?" The elementary school was a mile away from the high school, but I assumed people still talked.

Solemn, he chose his words carefully. "There was an incident, but it was nothing anyone would have killed him over." He paused. "The boy made a few mistakes. He spoke without thinking more often than not, and he got himself mixed up with the wrong crowd before he got married and settled down."

"You mean after I dumped him and he ran his mouth about me all over town?" There was no heat in my wry tone. I didn't blame Hudson for being upset at the way I handled things, and I couldn't tell my father I was going to have to pay penance for my actions by helping track down his murderer. "Anyone in that crowd a killer, do you think? Was he into anything dangerous?"

"I'd have said no, but circumstances being what they are, I might have misjudged. Just before the first Christmas after you left, Hudson showed up on the doorstep asking to borrow a hundred dollars to buy his mother a present. I loaned it to him, and he paid it right back on time, but later he admitted he'd lost the money in a high stakes—or what would be considered such in these parts—poker game run by Scooter Lowell."

I spent some time trying to pry more information out of him, but when my father decides to keep something secret, it goes in the vault never again to see the light of day.

He hit the button to close the garage door and couldn't help running a hand over the car's fender one last time before we headed outside and toward the house.

"Now, if you don't mind, I'm going to drag your mother away from cleaning and take her out for pizza. Tomorrow's the annual teacher's picnic, and I'm running the bingo game, so I'll send David over on Monday to inspect the attic."

The grin fell off my face. "You don't have to do that. I'm sure David has other things he'd rather be doing."

He used dad logic on me. "You wouldn't want your old man to lose sleep worrying about the state of things here, would you?"

Sigh. "No, I suppose not."

But I'd rather eat paste with a dirty spoon than have David skulking around in my attic.

"Fine, it's settled, then," Dad said, a victorious grin on his face. "I'm glad to have you home, but I'm sorry for how it happened. Love you, baby."

My emotional roller coaster stopped on the top of the hill when he folded his arms around me, and swayed a moment. "Love you, too, Daddy," I said, my reply muffled against the solid chest that had given solace from everything from skinned knees to moments of teenage angst, and now a failed marriage.

Taking my hand, he started up the steps. "Want me to go find that jerk and rough him up?"

Not in my wildest imagination could I dredge up a mental image of my peace-loving father putting a beat-down on Paul. My mother … yeah, that one came easy, but Dad wasn't the type.

"No, but thank you for the offer."

Late afternoon found Jacy slumped on one end of the sofa, and me on the other with our feet propped up on the coffee table.

"I'm starving," she announced.

I rolled my head to the left to give her a look. "I'm sweaty and dusty, and since dad mentioned pizza, I can't stop craving pepperoni."

With as minimal effort as she could manage, Jacy kicked off her shoes, then wiggled her toes and sighed with relief. "With peppers and onions, but no—"

"Mushrooms," we said in unison and exchanged a smile. "In a minute, I'll work up the energy to find my phone and call Hoppies." Our nickname for House of Pizza.

"Mine's closer. Okay with you if I call Bertino's instead? New place—well, they opened three years ago. They have this special sauce, it's ah-mazing. Spicy but sweet. I don't know what they put in it, but it has this sort of smoky flavor. Costs extra and you have to know about it to ask for it because it's not on the regular menu. You're going to love it."

Heaving my body off the sofa with an effort, I snagged Jacy's phone from the mantel and tossed it to her. "Sounds good to me. I'm going to go wash off a few layers of dirt. "

"Leave some hot water for me." Jacy had already punched in the number and had her phone to her ear.

Halfway through my shower, I took the first deep breath in days that didn't seem squashed by pain and anxiety. Moving forward, carving out the beginnings of a life for myself had begun to form a skin over the raw places left by cutting Paul out of my life. Or by him cutting me out of his. Though it came down to the same thing, I was determined to triumph, and not for the sake of proving anything to him. I would do this for me. I would make a home here, and it would be full of color and pattern and attitude.

With distance, I was coming to realize Paul could only shine if the things around him were too sterile and drab to compete, and I'd worked hard to blend in. But that was over. No more.

Never again.

CHAPTER 19

The chiming of a doorbell had never been so welcome. The delivery guy was the same one I'd seen at the gas station near the motel—Ray something or other. Had a kid who pitched for the baseball team.

My mouth watered at the smell wafting from the box, but I did the polite thing and refrained from snatching it out of his hand like some kind of animal.

"You Everly Dupree?" he asked.

"I am," I said, taking the box he'd removed from the insulated bag.

"Just need you to sign the slip."

I did as he asked and added a generous tip because the special sauce smelled better, if possible than the regular stuff I'd tried from the gas station already.

Like everyone else had for the past week, he looked at me with avid curiosity. "You're the one who found that poor fella at the motel. Damn shame."

I didn't want to talk about it, so I sidestepped that land mine and, proud of myself for remembering, asked about his son.

The change of topic brought a big grin to his face. "Tony's going to bring home the pennant for his team. Playoffs start tonight. I'm headed over to the field right now." He tucked the credit slip away and took his leave.

Riding my second, or maybe third, wind of the day, I popped the top on the Bertino's box. The first bite proved Jacy right. Hoppies had been outclassed.

"Until yesterday, I hadn't had pizza in almost two years," I confided and watched Jacy's eyes bug out.

"What? Are you kidding me?"

I shook my head, then picked a piece of pepperoni off my slice, watched the strings of cheese stretch long. "Paul refused to eat anything he deemed peasant food."

His weird eating rules hadn't really bothered me that much. I'd told myself I wasn't a picky eater, so whatever he'd wanted was fine with me. Except now that I didn't have to deal with him anymore, I realized it hadn't been fine.

"Don't take this the wrong way," Jacy said, waving her slice in my direction, "but you don't seem devastated by the break-up. Or are you putting on a brave face?"

If anyone else had asked me, I might have been able to skirt the question, but that never worked with Jacy. She knew me well enough to see through to the truth.

"Pieces of me still miss being married to the man I thought he was, but I'm coming to realize this divorce might be a lucky break for me." I took a swig of my drink. "But I don't want to think about him right now. Do you know anything about Scooter Lovell and a high-stakes poker game?

"I've heard rumors, but nothing more substantial. Why?"

"You didn't hear this from me, but I have it on good authority that Hudson lost some money to Scooter awhile back. Could be important."

Considering, Jacy slid another slice out of the box. "Do you think that's why someone killed him? Seems sorta like a lousy motive to me."

"It might be if the murder was premeditated, but I heard Ernie talking to one of the other officers that day, and they were saying it looked like a crime of opportunity. Maybe someone came for their money, and when he didn't have it, they argued, and it got heated, and then *bonk*. Ice bucket to the head."

"Ew," she said, scrunching her nose. "I'm trying to eat, you know."

But I was on a roll and couldn't stop. "It couldn't have been a woman, right? I mean Hudson used to play football, and he was still in pretty good shape." When Jacy cocked a brow at me, I said, "It's just a general observation. Seems like killing him would have taken a bit of strength."

"Or a solid wind up. Kind of like swinging a baseball bat. Or maybe they hid behind the door and took him by surprise."

I shook my head. "Then we're back to premeditation again, and if it had to do with gambling debts, I can't see anyone being dumb enough to think killing a man is a good way to get money out of him. Besides, there were defensive wounds. Ernie said so."

Shuddering, Jacy tossed the last rind of crust back into the box and flipped the lid. "Ernie will figure it out, and now that my belly isn't trying to eat me from the inside out, I'd like to stop talking about grisly things and look around here some more. Aren't you dying to see the upstairs? There's a tower room. I've always wanted a tower room. What do you think is in it?"

"Hard to say, but I'd put money on there being some type of fruit basket on the wallpaper."

Jacy snorted. "There does seem to be a theme to the decor."

The pink and blue ones in the kitchen might have been the busiest of Mrs. Willowby's choices downstairs, but she'd carried the motif throughout. Even in the parlor, the pattern of gold over an ecru background turned out to be an abstract version if you squinted when you looked at it.

"You think it was on purpose? Or did she just really love baskets of fruit? Who'd have ever thought there were so many different possibilities?"

The keys were all still on the kitchen table, and I still had the one for the garage in my pocket, so I put it in the pile of ones we'd already matched to doors.

"Same goes for door locks." I handed half the remaining keys to Jacy and trailed behind her as she practically bounced up the stairs.

The second-floor landing angled left into a dimly lit hallway with doors on both sides—all of them locked, naturally. Jacy had chosen the one she was sure led to the tower room and had already begun testing her keys in it when I stepped up beside her.

"Wait, let me see the lock." I hunkered down, rested a formerly clean knee on the dusty floor, and checked for the center pin like David had shown me. There was none. "None of those are going to work, they go to a different type of lock."

Jacy's face fell. "Well, shoot. It's a little like a treasure hunt, and I was hoping one of these was the key."

"Try these," I handed her several solid barrel keys. "See how there's no hole in the end? One of those should fit. Meanwhile, I'm going for door number two." I'd already spotted a pin-type lock across the hall.

Somehow, the testing of keys and the opening of doors turned into a race, and when I heard the snick of a turning key, I knew Jacy had won.

"Ooh, this is it. Look, Ev. See the stairs going up? I found the tower. I feel like Nancy Drew."

Gently nudging her out of the way, I took a look. "Looks dusty up there. I really don't want to take a third shower today. Maybe we should wait until the morning." It took everything I had to maintain a deadpan tone.

"Are you nuts? You stay down here if you want to, but you're not ruining this for me. If there's a bed up here, I might never come down."

"Okay, Rapunzel. I'm sure Brian will appreciate the nightly climb."

Flipping her hair and striking a pose, she said, "I'm totally worth it."

Laughing, I followed her up the stairs until she stopped dead near the top and I nearly banged my head on her butt.

"Whoa," was all she said.

"What? Get out of the way so I can see." When she didn't move, I pinched her calf, and she yelped.

"Ow! That wasn't nice." But she scaled the last two steps, and I finally got a look at the tower room.

The narrow space boasted a three-sided view and contained only four items. A tall chair, a matching table holding a small notebook, and a pair of binoculars.

"Oh, Mrs. Willowby. You were a nosy one. Look, you can see my place from here. We could signal each other by flashing the lights in Morse code."

The fact that I could picture us doing exactly that didn't stop me from teasing her. "Okay, Trixie Belden."

Jacy picked up the notebook and blew the dust off the top. "Shut up. You read the same books I did as a kid. What do you think is in here? A list of all the naughty things she saw?"

"Maybe." I'd moved closer to the front window, and the sight of Hudson's wife struggling to start her lawn mower had pulled my attention. "She looks so sad."

Joining me, Jacy looked down. The titillating possibilities in Catherine Willowby's notebook would have to wait. "We should go help her. It doesn't look like she has anyone else, and I heard Hudson's mother shut Neena out of everything to do with the funeral."

As we descended, Jacy carried the notebook as far as the hall table and dropped it there to be retrieved later.

Even in the subdued light of early dusk, I could see the glint of tears on Neena's face as she poked the priming bulb a few times, then yanked the starting cord on an older model push mower. The engine failed to start.

"Stupid piece of crap." She gave the machine a kick as we crossed the street. As far as I could tell, the lawn looked fine. Other than a couple of dandelion heads popping up, the grass could go at least a few more days before it would need cutting.

"Need some help?" I never know what to say in these situations, but one of Jacy's greatest assets was her ability to focus in on what was needed most. "We have this same model, and I know a trick to get it to start." Her easy manner and light tone were meant to put Neena at ease, and it worked. At least a little.

"I was hoping you were going to say you had a sledgehammer and we could bash it to smithereens." Neena's gaze cruised toward me. The way her posture stiffened slightly, I figured she expected me to bring up her recent tragedy. "Now that I'm on my own, I have all these things I have to learn to do. Mow the lawn, keep track of vehicle maintenance."

She gave the mower another kick. "Reporters hounding me for sound bites so they can dredge up fake sympathy for the poor widow of the murdered man. My husband is dead. He's *dead.* Someone killed him. I don't even know what to do with that information right now. It's too much to process. So I thought I'd find some mindless activity, something to blow off some steam. But no. Because this thing," another kick, "is a piece of crap."

"Tell her I love her." Hudson's voice sounded loud right next to my ear, and I jumped. We were going to have to talk about the rules sooner rather than later. I couldn't tell him to shut up without looking like an idiot, and I wouldn't give her his message for the same reason.

“Just like ours, the priming ball isn’t working anymore.” Jacy grabbed the handle and heaved the mower up on its left-hand side. She held it there for a moment and then dropped it back down. "Go ahead, give it a try now."

Looking skeptical, Neena did. Her expression turned to surprise when the engine sputtered to life. She let it run a few seconds, and when she let it die off, I made a note to buy some hearing protection before I mowed my lawn.

“I … thank you. I—” As if she’d been holding it in for a long time, a sob burst out of Neena. “I don’t … this is all so—”

Nearly crying herself, Jacy stroked a hand down the new widow’s arm, then pulled her in for a consoling hug. “I’m so sorry for your loss. We both are.” With an arm still around Neena’s shoulders, Jacy gently led the way to the front steps of the Montayne home and settled them both on the top one.

I added my own consolation while Hudson continued to badger me, and I did my best to ignore him. “Neena, are you dealing with all of this alone? Will anyone from your family be coming to stay?”

The question elicited another fresh spurt of tears, and I wished I’d never asked, but no one should go through such a grievous loss alone.

“There’s no one, and Hudson’s mother has taken over the arrangements for the funeral. She wouldn’t even let me pick out his suit. If she had her way, I wouldn’t be allowed to attend the service at all. She didn’t think I was good enough for her little saint, but she didn’t know everything about her son.”

Right now wasn’t time to offer my opinion of Hudson’s mother, especially with him standing right there. At least he’d stopped bugging me for the moment.

“I never thought my mother would do something like this. She and Neena butted heads, but then again, I never planned on dying and leaving the two of them alone. Tell Neena … tell her—” I didn’t know ghosts could choke up, but I guess you learn something new every day. “Never mind.” He paused, then said plaintively, “Listen Ev, I know I acted like an idiot coming on to you like I did, but I’d never have cheated on her. I just wanted you to think I would, and then I was going to turn you down cold. Give you a taste of your own medicine.”

Then who had he been banging the headboard with? My mouth popped open to ask, and I had to slam it shut to avoid making a fool of myself by asking stupid questions of thin air.

With half my attention focused on Neena and Jacy, I almost missed it when Hudson asked a favor of me. "Would you do something for me? Make friends with Neena. Be there for her even if it seems weird. She's a good woman, and she has no one else. I'll feel better if I know she's not alone. We have a history, you and me. You owe me that much. Say you will. Please."

Technically, I didn't owe him anything, and the favor I was already doing for him—or avoiding doing for him—should balance the scales for a lifetime. But Neena was hurting. Anyone with eyes could see her pain, and I wasn't about to take out my annoyed feelings for her dead husband on her. All I could do was nod and watch him fade away.

"If you want to take your mind off things for a few hours, I've moved into the house across the street, and we're exploring the upstairs rooms. We'd love to have you join us. I can't promise it will be fun, but I can guarantee you'll be distracted and dusty and probably need a shower when we're done."

Half a second after I blurted out the invitation, it occurred to me I hadn't said much to her up until now, and I probably came off as abrupt and a little awkward. Sorry, that's what happens when you're pestered by a ghost.

Bless Jacy, she piped up and smoothed things over.

"It looks like you could use some company right now, and Everly's right, taking your mind off your troubles might help them seem more manageable later. We'd totally understand if you feel like this isn't the right time for socializing, though. It's your call."

Whether she would have said yes or not, she never got the chance. Neena was still contemplating our offer when Ernie Polk cruised up the street and pulled into her drive. He had his official face on when he stepped out of the car.

"Mrs. Montayne. If I could have a moment." He swept a look over the three of us. "Everly. I wasn't aware you two ladies were acquainted."

It sounded like an accusation. "Everly is moving into the house across the street. She and Jacy were being neighborly." I hadn't expected Neena to stick up for me, but then, she might have taken his tone of voice as personally as I did. She didn't offer to invite Ernie inside, and he didn't ask, but I saw the curtains twitch at the house next door.

"We were headed over to my place anyway. Why don't you come inside and ask your questions away from prying eyes."

Neena shot me a nod of thanks, which I returned with the tiniest of smiles. If I wanted to get rid of Hudson, it looked like I was going to have to make friends with his widow. Fine by me. She seemed nice, and we were in similar boats.

Okay, hers was the Titanic and mine was a dinghy, but we were both survivors of shipwrecked marriages. I know that's a stupid metaphor, but I'd had a rough week.

Trailing behind, Jacy pushed the lawnmower inside and closed Neena's garage door. The skin on the back of my neck prickled like there were eyes on my back as I crossed the street with Neena. Dusk was on the edge of giving way to twilight as we stepped inside.

The long day of work following a sleepless night had not prepared me for a sudden bout of nerves. Did Ernie suspect me again? Or was it Neena who made his eyes go flat? Lord knew she had more reason to kill the man than I did.

Because the parlor was still crowded with unpacked boxes, I led my guests down the hall to the kitchen. "Can I get you anything? I could brew some coffee, or there are soft drinks in a cooler around here somewhere."

"It's on the porch. I'll be right back." Jacy gave me a look that I interpreted as an order to not let Ernie start without her. She wasn't gone a minute and returned with a couple of cans in each hand and a rueful look. "They're warm. The cover wasn't shut tight, and all the ice melted." She set them on the table, and when I went to get some glasses, directed me toward the dishwasher.

"No matter, we have plenty of ice."

"None for me, thanks," Neena said, her voice husky with emotion. "I don't like iced drinks. Neither did Hudson. It was one of the things we had in common."

Until she mentioned it, I'd forgotten that about him.

CHAPTER 20

"Reason I'm here is we found Hudson's truck." Ernie dropped the bombshell, and Neena sucked in a breath so hard I heard it whistle through her teeth. She didn't ask for details, so I did.

"Does that mean you found the person who …" I substituted a word for the one I'd been about to say "hurt him?"

"'Fraid not. Seems he sold the truck several hours before the attack." The way Ernie watched Neena's face was all the clue I needed to know there was more to the story.

Face burning red, Neena exploded. "Don't sugarcoat it. He sold the truck to pay off a gambling debt. Why didn't you come right out and ask me if I knew my husband was puttin' our money into card games? Of course, I knew. Why do you think he was living at the Bide A Way?"

Dryly Ernie replied, "You did say you had marital differences, and he *was* catting around. I put two and two together right enough."

"You put two and two together and came up with six, you mean. What makes you think my husband was catting around?"

All it took was for Ernie to glance my way, and the heat of Neena's fury turned toward me.

Holding up my hands, I protested. "Wait. I wasn't sleeping with Hudson. For one, I don't sleep with married men, and two, I've sworn off all men for the foreseeable future. Frankly, and this is no reflection on you, Ernie, but I'm not a fan of the gender at the moment."

Neena's gaze never wavered.

"Okay, I admit I did tell Ernie I heard Hudson, um … well … he had someone in the room. I'm sorry, Neena. I would have told you about it, but there hasn't really been a good time." Nothing on this earth would drag the admission that he'd hit on me from my lips. Not when his ghost had admitted he hadn't meant to go through with anything.

The very last thing I expected was for Neena's face to break out in a tight smile. "Oh honey, I know you weren't sleeping with Hudson. My honey was a one-woman man. I kicked him out to teach him a lesson, but that didn't mean I couldn't pay him a visit, if you know what I mean."

"Can you blame me? Just look at her." Hudson popped in behind Ernie and almost made me spit my drink.

Oblivious to the specter hovering over him, Ernie pressed his lips into a thin, disapproving line, and amended his notes.

"Let me get this straight. You're saying you were with Hudson on the night of his death?"

"Sure was."

"And you didn't think to tell me this before? I could make a case against you for providing false information."

She rolled her eyes. "Now, Ernie. You know I didn't lie. You never asked me that. Not specifically. You asked when he was home last, but you never came right out and asked me about the last time I'd seen him."

This time, Ernie was the one whose face burned red. "It was inferred."

"Implied," Jacy corrected automatically, and Ernie huffed out an exasperated sound.

He rectified the mistake and grilled Neena on her movements as they pertained to the night of Hudson's murder. After leaving her husband sated and satisfied, Neena had stopped at the Gas N Go for gas and a Payday bar.

"I always get hungry. You know … after."

"That's my girl." Hudson crowed. "Built for speed and got a tiger in the tank."

That was more information than I really wanted, and what's more, it was being given behind Neena's back. Sort of.

Ernie took Neena back and forth over her story several times, but she didn't budge an inch in the retelling, so he moved on to the matter of Hudson's truck.

"Here's a copy of the bill of sale, and I've never known Millard Davidson to lie. If he says Hudson sold him the truck, I believe him."

"He probably did," Neena said. "It doesn't surprise me in the least."

Hudson poofed before Neena baldly explained how the loss of his head coaching position had pushed him into a downward spiral that ended with him gambling away most of their savings. What she failed to explain was what had cost him the job. It seemed Ernie already knew, so he didn't let any details slip, either.

"That's your marital difference," she told Ernie. "I won't live with a betting man. Especially one who wagers more than he can afford, and Hud couldn't seem to help himself." Given the shadows haunting her eyes, I suspected her husband wasn't the first man in her life with a similar weakness.

Having stayed quiet longer than I'd ever known her to, Jacy was the one who asked, "How'd he lose his job?"

Neena's shoulders rounded as she huddled in on herself. "I love my husband, but sometimes the man was dumber than a sackful of tree stumps. One of the basketball players got hit upside the head with a weighted ball during practice. Pure accident and no one could argue the point, but the boy had a concussion. It was the final game of the tourney, and being a senior, it woulda been the boy's last game before graduating, so he begged and said he'd tell his folks it happened after the game, not before, and Hudson gave in and let him play."

I couldn't determine from her tone exactly how Neena felt about what had happened, but there was no denying it had been a stupid thing to do.

"The boy ended up in the ER that night, and it all came out. The kid stood up for Hudson, so he only got bumped down to assistant coach even though the parents wanted him fired. This is all closed-door information, so y'all please, promise me you'll keep it quiet. Hudson's gone now. There's no need of draggin' his name through the mud."

She didn't name names, but I wondered if Ernie considered the boy or his father a suspect. I added both to my list and contemplated again whether there was a way Hudson's gambling debts might play into his death. At least the suspect pool was now bigger than a guppy bowl.

When Ernie left a half hour after he'd arrived, he had more information than he'd started with, but very little of it helpful.

Neena stood and smoothed her hands down the front of her cotton blouse, then adjusted the set of her shoulders. "What about those rooms we were going to explore?" There was a false note of cheer in her voice and a pleading look in her eyes that made me think she wasn't in the mood for more questions. What she needed was a distraction, and we'd offered to provide her with one.

"I'll get the keys." Jacy sprang into action. How she still had any spring left in her was beyond me. I felt like I'd been tied to a car antenna and driven down the highway for an hour. She seemed bright and daisy-fresh when she laid the keys on the table.

"All the rooms downstairs use this one," she pointed to a key with a solid shaft. "That one opens all the closet doors on this level." Also a solid shaft, but a thinner one than the first. "That's the basement key, the wide one with the pinhole in the end, and this one opens the tower door."

Jacy looked up and caught me grinning at her. "What? I worked it out after you told me about the pins." She picked up the three remaining keys. "By process of elimination, this one probably opens all the doors on the second floor, this one the closets, and," she pointed to the most ornate, "that one probably goes to the attic—if there is one."

Neena snatched up the closet key and headed toward the stairs with Jacy hard on her heels. "Let's go find out if there are any skeletons in Mrs. Willowby's closets. I'm itchin' to see."

I could have happily tumbled into bed, but if pawing around in dusty closets would give Neena some peace, I'd go along with it.

Oh, who was I kidding? I wanted to know what kind of pig was in my poke.

"This is excitin'. It's like being on a game show and getting to pick between door number one or door number two." Neena stood in the hallway and surveyed her options. There were a lot more than just the two doors to choose from, but it looked like she was taking her time.

Jacy pointed. "These old houses, some of the closets opened out into the hallway. See how this door is narrower? And that one over there, too."

Waiting for them to choose was like watching someone pick away at the wrapping on a gift in order to save the paper. I'm of the *tear it off and see what's inside* persuasion.

Finally, Neena fitted a key to the lock of her choice and, angling her body so she would have the best view, gave the key a twist. The door swung open, she leaned in for a peek, let out a yelp, and slammed it shut again.

My heart took the express route to my shoes and grabbed my stomach to go along for the ride.

"What? What is it? It better not be an actual skeleton." Yet, I was in no rush to see.

Putting a hand to her cheek, Neena turned toward us—Jacy had stepped to my side and was now clutching my hand like it was a lifeline.

"Not exactly, but close." Neena turned the handle and pulled the door wide.

In perfect unison, Jacy and I looked at the contents and then at each other. Horror gave way to the kind of giggles that come when you're faced with the absurd on a day when you're already feeling punchy from lack of sleep.

At first, Neena stared at us, then she cracked a smile. Pretty soon all three of us were howling, which was probably inappropriate since her husband hadn't even been put in the ground. Stress comes out in funny ways sometimes.

"What on earth was she going to do with a closet full of mannequin heads?" I couldn't hazard a guess at the answer, but there they were, all bald and staring with their creepy eyes—jammed in among sets of arms and legs.

"Where are the bodies?" Jacy wiped away tears of laughter.

Neena wrapped her arms around her middle and tried to catch her breath. "Probably in the other closet."

"Looks like a squirrel putting away nuts for the winter, only it's heads." The laughter made me wheezy, but it also released another layer of the tension I'd been carrying for days.

Jacy held her hand out for the key, and when Neena passed it over, tried the second closet. "I'm sorry, but I have to know."

"There ought to be a soundtrack playing in the background," Neena said. "Dun dun dun."

With a flourish, Jacy drew open the door to reveal not torsos but coats. A lot of coats—all of them preserved in plastic covers. The closet held a few cobwebs and a history lesson in winter outerwear.

“Oh, this is better than a mannequin body any day of the week.” Jacy pulled out and unzipped the bag holding a sassy pink swing coat circa 1956. “It’s in perfect condition. I just love it.” She held it out for Neena to play fingers along the soft material.

Don’t get me wrong, I like fashion as much as the next woman, but my butt was dragging and my energy was just about gone. I didn’t have it in me to gush over a bit of pink wool at that moment. Not even if it was fine cashmere.

Trying not to seem like I was rushing them along, I gently persuaded my companions to put the coat away, and we went downstairs to settle in the living room. With their soft voices rising and falling around me, I tipped my head back and slid into a doze.

CHAPTER 21

Until Jacy gently shook me awake, I'd been indulging myself in a dream where Mrs. Willowby, the younger version from her photographs, welcomed me to her home and said she wanted me to make myself at home there.

Since I already planned to do just that, I figured the dream for a bout of anxiety relief.

"C'mon, Ev. You can't spend the night sleeping on the sofa. It sets a bad precedent."

I think I grunted something in response because my tongue felt thick, and so did my brain.

Jacy—who looked almost as tired as me by then—took the left-hand side of the bed, and if there was a race to unconsciousness, I couldn't say who won.

I was the first one up in the morning, so I dragged myself to the kitchen to see if I could rustle up a pot of coffee. My bare toes tested the texture of the vinyl flooring, and I caught myself smiling in spite of the eye-watering wallpaper. I could see myself cooking meals in this room, slowly arranging things to my preferences, settling into a solitary, but fulfilling lifestyle.

If Catherine Willowby could be happy here alone, so could I.

Slowly, I took the tour of the cupboards. Since my mom and Jacy had done the bulk of the cleaning in this room, I wasn't entirely certain where they'd stashed the coffeemaker. Or, for that matter, if there was one.

"You didn't tell Neena I love her." Hudson materialized next to me and scared me half out of my skin.

"What have I said about just showing up like that?" I hissed in case Jacy woke up.

He ignored the question. "Why didn't you tell her?"

"Because, you idiot, I can't tell her that without letting her know you're haunting me, and she's got enough on her plate right now without me freaking her out even more. It's not like you went out peacefully in your sleep, you know."

During the whispered conversation, I kept up the search for a coffeepot, and also maintained a listening ear in case Jacy stirred. I didn't need her thinking I'd gone over to the woo-woo side, and if she caught me talking to Hudson, I'd have to tell her about him.

As if he read my mind, Hudson said, "You missed it."

"Missed what?"

He pointed to the cabinet door I'd just closed. "That tall pot with the glass bulb in the lid. That's a percolator."

I cocked an eyebrow at him.

"For coffee." He carefully avoided touching me, but when I opened the cabinet in question, pointed to the item in question.

"This makes coffee?"

"Jeez, Ev. Not everyone uses drip makers. She's got a French press in there, too, if you like a more full-bodied brew."

What was he? Some kind of coffee expert?

"All I want is a cup of coffee sometime in the next fifteen minutes. Which one of these things can make that happen and how?"

Under his direction, I filled the percolator, added coffee to the basket, and fired up the stove.

"You weren't fooling around on Neena." I made it a statement, not a question, and put some warmth into my voice because that was information that made me more willing to help him. As if I had a choice.

"No. And she didn't kill me, either. I might not know who did, but I know it wasn't her."

Just as I started to ask him about the gambling, I heard footsteps in the hall and ordered him to go. He grinned and faded just as Jacy walked into the kitchen.

"Is that coffee I smell?"

"It's an attempt. Have you ever used one of these?" I gestured to the percolator.

"No, but it smells amazing in here. I'm starving."

We hadn't fully stocked the kitchen during our shopping trip the day before, but I'd had the forethought to grab eggs and sausage for the morning. Working together, we cooked breakfast and chatted about colors for the room.

“Yellow, I think. I like the sheer curtains because they let in the light. I want it to be bright and cheerful. Other than the wallpaper, it’s a great room already.”

Jacy expertly slid over-easy eggs on a plate, set it near my coffee, then added one for herself while I buttered toast for us both.

We ate in silence for the first few minutes, then Jacy said, “Did you see the light fixture over the sink?”

“How could I miss it? It looks like a flying saucer.”

"Check this out." Rising and going over to the sink, Jacy reached up and grasped a knob that looked like it held the glass in place. She pulled down and then pushed up, and the whole fixture turned out to be adjustable. "How cool is that? That's some space-age tech that was ahead of its time."

“Still looks like a flying saucer, though.”

When we’d finished and stashed our dishes in the dishwasher, I let her talk me into cleaning the hallway and checking at least one more room upstairs before she went home for the day and left me to finish unpacking.

With her wielding the vacuum and me following behind with rag and mop, we cleared up our dusty footprints from the day before. The closet full of mannequin heads, we left alone since the coat closet hadn’t turned out to need much cleaning.

I let Jacy choose which room to open, but I did the honors and turned the key in the lock. Would there be a bedroom on the other side of the door? Or a roomful of who knew what? The only way to find out was to look, and so I threw the door open wide.

“Oh, Jace.” My breath caught. Dustier than any room so far, it looked like the fully outfitted nursery had been closed up for far longer than the year or so since Mrs. Willowby’s death. “This is the saddest thing I’ve ever seen.”

Long abandoned webs now carried dust instead of spiders and looped in dark and lacy strands from the light fixture in the center to a crib that had only ever held a mother’s hope. Worse, knowing Jacy possibly faced the same state of childlessness, my heart broke for the feelings this sight must have evoked in her.

"That poor woman," was all she said, but when I closed the door, Jacy didn't ask to open another, and she hadn't fully regained her bubbly spirit when she left an hour later.

Alone, finally, in my new home, I stood and listened to the quiet. There had been sorrow here, but I knew there had also been joy.

Somewhat sobered by the realization, I spent the next hour just wandering through the open rooms and out into the backyard I'd only seen from a distance so far. From the back side of the house, the addition looked much larger than I'd expected, hidden as parts of it were by the main house when standing out front.

Curious, I went back inside and tested a couple of the keys in the lock on the door to the addition. When none of them fit, I debated trying a few more, but decided to save some of the surprises for later and strolled around the downstairs making lists of what I needed to do to make myself comfortable in the house first.

It would have been nice if Hudson had shown up once I was alone, but of course, he did not. That would have been too convenient.

Finally, after a slice of leftover pizza, I raided Mrs. Willowby's VCR tape collection and settled in with the rest of Jacy's ice cream and a comedy movie marathon until it was time for bed. I was worried I wouldn't sleep since it was my first night in the house alone, but once my head hit the pillow, I never heard a thing until my alarm went off.

CHAPTER 22

Ten minutes early for my first day at work, I stood outside the office and gave myself a little speech about how this was a great chance to learn new skills and that I could totally handle whatever Spencer threw at me. Then, armed with the confidence of my convictions, I went inside.

As it turned out, I was right. He stationed me in a smaller office I hadn't noticed before and showed me what he needed me to do for the day.

"We have seven mortgages in the works right now," he said. "This is a typical week for us since we're basically the last resort for folks with bad credit, and we service the tri-county area."

Gesturing for me to take a seat, he leaned over me to pull up a folder of email. "I need you to go through the unread emails from the underwriters and compile a list for each case number of what documents are needed. Check to see if the applicants have already been asked to provide the information and if they've responded. If so, get the documents emailed to whoever asked for them. Otherwise, send out new requests and then stay on top of responses."

So far, it sounded easy enough.

"Keep your lists updated as the documents are sent and watch the email for incoming requests. If anything is kicked back for whatever reason by the underwriters, forward it along to me, and I'll take it from there."

"Okay, I'm sure I can handle that."

Spencer shot me a smirk that said he might not share my opinion of my abilities. "You probably won't get responses on everything today, but we're a little behind. I'll expect the backlog to be cleared by noon."

Because I wasn't fond of that look, I vowed internally to have it done by eleven and scrolled back to find the earliest unopened email, which was dated nearly a week before. A little behind was a massive understatement.

The work, though, was not that difficult, and I took advantage of the email program's canned responses feature to set up a few basic templates to send to applicants that halved the time it took for each request for information.

When I emerged at eleven fifteen, I'd not only cleared the backlog but also all the new requests for the morning. Most of the applicants had acknowledged the request or provided the needed documents. A great result considering some of the dates on the original requests were from more than a week prior.

Spencer, however, wasn't given to praise for a job well done. Instead, he sent me back to my computer with instructions on where to find the rejected deals folder and asked me to draft emails to hopeful mortgage applicants and inform them they weren't qualified for a loan at this time.

Knowing I was dashing someone's dream of home ownership, I was happy to see there were only two of them. One for a young couple with no credit history, and the other for a man named Ray Watson who had been trying to arrange a second mortgage on a home without enough equity.

That one drew a full-on rant of a reply. It seemed Mr. Watson had already been notified of his denial and did not appreciate the follow-up on my part.

At noon, I took my lunch break, and then, when I went to ask what I should do next, realized Spencer had left the office without giving me any further instructions.

Robin, the cheerless woman who answered phones, confirmed he wouldn't return and only shrugged when I asked what I was supposed to do for the rest of the day, and so I went back to my office and waited for more email to come in.

Not much later, she poked her head in the open door and said, "I'm out of here."

Since that, filing her nails, and reading magazines seemed to be the only things she did, I figured it couldn't be too difficult. "When do we close? Is there a key so I can lock up?"

I hadn't seen any official hours posted anywhere, which was a little odd, but Spencer had said he got almost all of his clients from the Internet, so maybe he wasn't keeping to a strict schedule. Still, it would have been nice to know what my hours would be. For that matter, I realized we hadn't discussed my salary beyond what he was offering me for a two-week trial. At the end of that time, he'd said, I'd either be hired or let go depending on my performance.

Given Robin's lack of such, I didn't see a huge problem.

She returned a moment later with a key and dropped it on my desk. “There’s a key. Knock yourself out.”

Was it some kind of test?

I shot Spencer an email asking what he wanted me to do, and since all office email went out with return notifications, knew he’d opened my message, but he didn’t bother to answer.

What a jerk. If there had been any other job offered, I'd have taken it instead of this one. Scrubbing toilets might have been preferable to being left in the office with no idea what to do. An hour passed, and I'd just about decided to go and take my lumps if I got fired when the phone rang.

I picked up the receiver and didn't even have a chance to say anything when I heard a gruff male voice. "Hey Bobbin Robin, tell him the heat's on, so I moved the Thursday night game to Tuesday, and we're gonna be at Bandy's. 9 pm. Back door."

“I’m not—”

Click. Too late. Scooter Lovell had hung up, but he’d given me some valuable information first. If I wanted to talk to him, I knew exactly where he’d be come Tuesday night.

Had Spencer and Hudson been friendly? Or maybe they’d been poker rivals—if that was even a thing, most of my knowledge of the game came from TV and movies where shady people smoked cigars and assessed each other from under beetled brows.

Still, to get to Bandy’s, I was going to need a driver or my own wheels, so I called Mrs. Tipton and asked about the car I’d sorta inherited.

"I guess since the town was granted the property in probate, we could sign the title over to you, and it would be all legal." I wasn't sure she sounded entirely confident. "Do you know where the title is? If you can find it and get here before we close, I'm happy to do up the paperwork."

The only way that was going to happen was if I left work now.

Figuring I wouldn't be more than five minutes away and could come back if the underwriters or applicants needed me, I set up the email to forward to my phone, and closed up shop. No one else seemed to care about being there, and since I wasn't being paid hourly, I'd take my chances.

Mom had pointed out a plastic filing bin in one of my kitchen cabinets. She'd only glanced through its contents quickly, but it held all the receipts and instruction booklets for the appliances and whatnot, so I hoped it contained other paperwork as well. Otherwise, I'd have to turn the house upside down looking for the title to the car.

I heard the lawnmower and saw the tail end of David's truck when I turned down my street. I'd forgotten he was planning to come and mow again. Or that dad had asked him to take a look at the attic. By my watch, I had less than an hour to make it to the town office with the paperwork on the car, and wrangling with David dropped down a notch on my priority list.

He saw me fumbling with the key and waved but kept on mowing. Already cloudy, the day threatened to turn wet, so I assumed he was trying to play beat the clock. Churlish as I felt around him, I had to admit the lawn looked less like a hayfield than it had.

Inside, I made a mad dash for the filing bin and set it up on the table to leaf through the contents. About halfway through, I hit pay dirt with a folder labeled: Car. Not only was the title there, but she'd maintained meticulous records of its upkeep.

Snatching up the title and the car keys, I headed for the garage.

"What are you doing?" I hadn't heard the mower shut off, but there was David standing right outside the door as it rolled up. He stepped inside and planted himself in front of the Buick.

I spared him a glance as I popped open the glove box and searched for the registration. "I'm going to the town office to get this thing registered. A girl's gotta have wheels."

"It's not registered or inspected. That's a double ticket if you get pulled over. Better let me take you."

I didn't have time to argue with him, but it didn't look like he planned to move out of the way, either.

“Fine, let’s go before Mrs. Tipton leaves for the day.” I pulled out my phone, leaned in, and snapped a shot of the mileage indicator. “I’m ditching work for this, so I need to get it done and get back before I end up getting fired.”

Okay, that was a mixture of truth, and stuff I wasn't sure was the truth. Still, I appreciated that he didn't resort to small talk during the short drive. Nor did he offer to accompany me inside, but his voice sounded pleasant enough when he said, "You go ahead, I'll wait right here."

Mrs. Tipton asked me about the house while she sorted through the documents I’d brought. “I’ll need proof of insurance, but everything else looks in order. There might be time if you run over to Smith Agency for a quote while I get everything underway.”

"Thanks, Mrs. T, but it's the digital age. There's an app for that." By the time she had the new registration and title application made up, an ID card had hit my inbox, and I was finalizing the process of getting a quote on the house.

"My daughter bought me one of those smarty-pants phones," Mrs. Tipton said. "She hooked me up to the Twitter and the Facebank. No, Facebook. Land sakes. What a rat's nest that turned out to be. Why everyone on God's green earth thinks they need to blast out their opinion on every little thing is beyond me."

I leaned my elbows on the counter and gave her a smile. As far as I was concerned, Mrs. Tipton was magic, and if she didn’t want to Tweet her personal business, it wouldn’t change my opinion one single bit. Since I’d come to town, she’d managed to get me into a house and put me behind the wheel of a car inside of a week.

“Thank you, Mrs. Tipton. You’re a treasure. In fact, I think you might just be my fairy godmother.”

“Go on, you cheeky girl. I only did my job.” But her face had pinked up with pleasure at the compliment.

Not even having David waiting for me could wipe the grin off my face, and if I wasn’t mistaken, old sourpuss cracked a tiny smile when I bounced into the seat beside him carrying my new license plates and registration.

One more step toward my new life.

House. Check.

Job. Check.

Car. Check.

Or nearly, as David had pointed out. I still needed to get the car inspected before it was fully legal.

Hudson's voice nearly sent me out the window. "Take it to my buddy Bennie over at Pine Tree Auto. He knows the car already. Slap a sticker on it in no time."

Not only could Hudson pop up whenever and wherever he pleased, but little things like the laws of physics didn't make a dent in his ability to hover half in and half out of a moving pickup truck.

"Matter of fact, he doesn't close up before five, and he's got a thing for the ladies. Flirt with him a little, and he'll get you right in. The car doesn't need anything, and he knows it hasn't been driven much."

I felt David's eyes on me as Hudson faded back out, and I tried not to react. But I'd sucked in a breath when he'd shown up, and probably twitched enough to draw attention besides.

To cover, I pulled out my phone and checked my email again. No new messages from work, and when we'd passed, I hadn't seen Spencer's car out front, so I was probably safe enough on that front.

But still, David watched me more than he seemed to watch the road.

"Listen, thanks for the ride." The first drops of rain pattered gently against the windshield. "You don't need to hang around and look at the attic today. Or ever, for that matter. My dad can be a little pushy at times, only you don't even notice what's happening until it's too late. He flashes those puppy dog eyes and the next thing you know, you're falling right into place."

That time I know I saw his mouth twitch.

"It's a finely honed skill, but it works every time. I'm just glad he only uses his powers for good." The last thing I wanted David to do was think I was making fun of my dad. "Imagine what would happen if he decided to go into politics."

"I think the world would be a better place if men like your father were running things."

There was a deep level of admiration in his tone. Enough to drag my defenses against him to a lower point. "Agreed." We'd pulled into my drive by that time. "Again, I appreciate the ride, and I don't want to seem rude, but if it's at all possible to get the car inspected today, I have to run. Raincheck on the attic?"

"Tomorrow afternoon. I'll be by after I'm done for the day."

"It's a date." Panic. "I mean a plan. Not a date. I'm never dating again. Not ever." Shoving the door open, I practically tumbled out onto the ground in my haste to get away from an awkward situation.

And that time he laughed right out loud. "Somehow I doubt that, but I'll come by around five. We still need to have that talk."

Already headed toward the garage, I waved a hand over my shoulder in dismissal.

CHAPTER 23

I didn't need to use my womanly wiles on Bennie, and I wouldn't have done so in any case. It seemed a grapevine tendril had already snaked its way into his shop. He met me at my car door.

"You must be Everly Dupree." Hudson had been wrong about him. I wasn't sure whether to be annoyed or relieved, but Bennie only had eyes for the Buick.

"I am. Have we met?" I didn't remember him, but that wasn't a sure sign of anything.

"No, Ma'am, but I did hear you'd bought Miss Catherine's place, and this is her car, so I put two and two together. I take it you're putting her back on the road." Smudges of grease and grime had settled into the grooves on his face, but Bennie's brown eyes sparkled kindly. "They don't make them like this anymore."

"Isn't that the truth. That's the plan. Do you have time to give her a quick inspection?" Why were cars referred to as she or her? Maybe this one was a dude.

His face clouded over, and I thought he was going to say no. "You were the one who found Hudson dead." It wasn't a question, but I nodded anyway.

"I was."

"Good man, Hudson. He used to come out and help me once in a while. Wouldn't take a penny for it. I can't figure out why anyone would want to kill him like that." Bennie reached for my keys, then thought the better of it. "Pull her right in. Won't take a minute."

While Bennie set the arms of his lift in place, I said, "Had Hudson helped you recently?"

"Naw, but he did come in and put a new set of brakes on his truck before he sold it."

I waited until the high pitched buzz of the air impact gun wound down, and Bennie rolled my front wheel out of the way.

"I bet he hated to see it go."

"Had me looking out for a replacement. Something he could fix up, but wouldn't cost too much to buy. Needed the money to pay off some debts."

That jived with what Ernie had said.

"Was he being threatened? You know, to pay off the money he owed?"

My wheel went back on before Bennie replied. "Not like you mean. Scooter Lovell would take an old lady's dentures as payment if he thought he could make a buck off them, but he ain't no killer or nothing."

A stellar character reference if I'd ever heard one.

"Do you know anything about the trouble he had at work?"

Before he answered, Bennie raised my car up higher and inspected the exhaust. Enough time passed that I'd decided he either didn't know or wasn't going to tell any of his friend's secrets.

"He made a stupid decision, but it come out of knowing how a boy might grow up to be a man and wonder if he'd lost his chance at one of his finest moments in life because he didn't get to play that last game. 'Specially since it mighta been his last one ever."

While Bennie flicked the lights on and off and tested the horn, I put two and two together and decided to make a stop at the grocery store on my way home.

On the plus side, with an acre of trunk space, I could stock the kitchen in a single trip.

"You coming to the funeral tomorrow?" Bennie had finished attaching my new sticker and was writing up the bill.

I hadn't even considered it, though I should have. Should I go? Hudson's mother wasn't exactly thrilled with me, though I didn't credit her threat as anything more than the lashing out of a distraught woman. Plus, I'd been the one to find him, and even though Ernie wasn't looking at me as a suspect—or at least I didn't think he was—others might. Especially if Viola Montayne had anything to say about it.

Confronting her might have been on my to-do list, but her son's funeral didn't seem like the right time or place to check it off.

"No, I think I'd better not."

"I think you'd better rethink your decision." Having Hudson pop up unexpectedly was becoming the norm, and for once, I wasn't even startled. "Whoever killed me might be there, and you're not doing a whole lot to figure out who that is."

"Thanks, Bennie." I paid, and with Hudson following behind, got in my car and backed out of the garage bay.

As soon as we cleared hearing distance, I inhaled and then lit into him. "You have to stop showing up like that. Can't you see that man is mourning your loss? And I'm doing the best I can. In case you haven't noticed, my life has taken a turn for the weird and not everything I'm dealing with revolves around you."

I might as well have been talking to thin air.

"Sorry."

He wasn't.

"Getting you to move on is a priority in my life. Trust me, there's nothing I want more. But it's not like you've been super helpful, and I'm not exactly equipped to be tracking down a murderer. What do you think I'm supposed to do if I figure it out who it was? Hmm?"

He ran his fingers through his hair. "I don't know, Ev. I don't know." Then he was gone.

Navigating the grocery store aisles, I returned the few curious glances tossed my way with smiles. Let them wonder about me, let them speculate, but damned if I was going to hang my head in shame I hadn't earned.

Not even when Miss Flippity Do from the employment office scanned me up and down, noted my professional attire, and cocked an eyebrow. Just for fun, I walked right over to her and said, "Well, hello Carlene. It's good to see you again."

"I … uh … hello Everly. Still job hunting?"

"No, I found something." Unless leaving early meant today was my first and last day, but she didn't have to know that, did she? And so what if I did get fired. Jacy was right, I could open a B&B if I had to, or maybe start some kind of shop out of my house. I didn't really want people running tame in my living space, but I decided, right there in aisle three of the grocery store, I'd do what I had to do to stand on my own two feet.

"If you'll excuse me, I have a lot of shopping to do." With that, I pushed my cart toward the produce section where I planned to buy a head of iceberg lettuce.

Oh, I know that doesn't sound like something you'd do to declare your independence, but I'd been living with a man who had vastly strange ideas of what constituted acceptable foodstuffs. And while I liked romaine just fine, I didn't think there was a single thing wrong with making a nice cob or wedge salad out of a crisp head of iceberg lettuce. Perfect with the pork chops that would round out my utter disdain for Paul's finicky meal choices. Those I added to a cart already full of basic staples like flour, sugar, spices, and the kind of tea I preferred.

At the checkout, I got behind a couple of men, one carrying a twelve pack of beer and the other a bag of beef jerky.

"Ten bucks says the Watson kid pitches a no-hitter," Beer guy said.

Jerky dude swiped his forearm to wipe across his nose. "Nope. Fool's bet. Kid's got a hell of an arm on him. Gonna take the state title this year. Last time we brought home the pennant—"

"Yeah, I know. You was the big hero sliding into home base. I've heard this one a thousand times."

"Everyone's heard it." Smiling to take the sting out of the words, the clerk rang up the beer and jerky.

When it was my turn, I made polite sounds to the clerk and picked up the donation box with the boy's photo on it.

Now that I was paying attention, I recognized the car he was leaning againt. Same blue sedan, same dented fender, and even though only the E and an L were visible, I'd lay money I'd seen that bumper sticker before.

The day I'd come back to town, that car had been parked in front of Hudson's room at the Bide A Way.

I committed the boy's name to memory. I also added another couple of dollars to the collection just in case the search for answers to Hudson's death turned up something that would make his life even more difficult.

Neena sat on my top step when I got home looking pale and angry.

"Do you know what that witch went and did?" Rightly assuming she meant Hudson's mother, I was glad not to be the one on the receiving end of her temper.

“Look! Just look at this!” She handed me the newspaper clipping of Hudson’s obituary. “She called the paper and had them remove my name.”

If I'd said I was surprised at Viola's hubris, it would be a flat lie. Nothing she could do would shock me. Absolutely nothing. Neena ranted for a minute or two, then she just sort of ran down like a wind-up toy and ended huddled with her head on her knees.

“Come inside,” I said, motioning for her to stand. “You need a friendly face and a cup of tea.”

"You're only half right unless tea is a euphemism for hard liquor, and then you're bang on the money."

I settled her at the table, put the kettle on to boil, and went back out for the groceries. From the look of her, Neena needed a few minutes in a safe space. I couldn’t imagine it was easy living with Hudson’s things all around, and having to deal with his mother on top of everything else was enough to try a saint’s patience.

Neena didn’t strike me as the patient type as, watching me over the brim, she blew on her tea to cool it enough to drink.

"What am I supposed to do now?" The question burst out of her, and I knew she wasn't just talking about the funeral. "I sent him to that motel to teach him a lesson."

By banging the headboard on the wall? I bit my tongue before the question popped out of my mouth.

"You're not the only one with regrets, you know. I clapped a pillow over my head and went back to sleep. If I'd stayed up a little longer, I might have heard the scuffle."

Sorrow in her eyes, Neena said, “Coulda, woulda, shoulda. And in the end, it was Hudson’s fate.”

My aunt had meant the world to me, and when she’d passed, I’d tried to believe it was fate, or destiny, or her time. Or any one of the other comments people make when they're trying to understand why tragedy falls down on this person or that person and misses them.

I took a deep breath and decided to come clean with her about running into him before he died. “I found him walking that evening and gave him a ride to the motel that night. He must have been coming back from selling the truck. I’d like to say we had some deep and meaningful conversation about some sort of epiphany he’d had, but we didn’t. Mostly, I apologized for being a typical teenager and breaking up with him in a way that nicked his ego so hard he carried a grudge. He forgave me, and …" The next part was a lie, but only a white one. "… he told me how much he loved you."

I couldn't exactly tell her his ghost had asked me to tell her that, but at least I was able to give her the truth of his words, if not in their proper context. His attempt to pay me back for hurting him was a secret no one ever needed to hear, and especially not Neena.

Some women cry beautifully, their eyes drenched in tears, their faces a mask of sorrow. Neena was not one of those women. She cried like a toddler who could see the lollipop on the table but wasn't able to reach it.

"He told me he'd sold the truck and paid off the gambling debt, and he begged me to let him come home. I wanted to make sure he was good and properly sorry for his actions, and I said no. His mother's right. I shouldn't even go to the funeral."

"Viola's lashing out because she's hurting, and she's not known for being the most rational or kind person, even at the best of times. Hudson would want you at his funeral. That much I know. He loved you."

Sniffling, she nodded. "Will you go with me? I don't have family, and I'm clearly not going to be part of Hudson's anymore. I think I could get through it if I didn't feel so terribly alone."

How was I supposed to say no to her?

"Yes. I'll go." Internally, I sighed. "For now, why don't you stay awhile? I'm going to cook some pork chops and make a salad. Nothing fancy, but I'd love the company."

CHAPTER 24

As much as I'd looked forward to a quiet evening, Neena had needed me more, and she'd stayed late, which meant I dragged myself out of bed the next morning with reluctance and got ready for work.

Robin waggled her fingers at me when I came in, but didn't bother to look up from her magazine. I'd left the message about the poker game on her desk because I didn't want to be the one to relay it to Spencer.

"He in?" The door was closed, but that wasn't a sign of anything.

"Not yet."

"Is there something I'm supposed to be doing to assist him? He hasn't really given me enough information to know the scope of the job."

Why I was asking Miss Bubblegum this question was a mystery to me. She merely shrugged and left me to wonder why he felt the need to hire me. It wasn't like Robin was overworked or the work too complicated. Why wasn't she handling the underwriter requests?

Pondering a less than charitable answer to that question, I went into my office and checked the inbox. Less than an hour of relaying underwriter requests to applicants and forwarding along the responses from the day before cleared it completely.

When I went to check, Spencer was in his office.

"Got a minute?"

He glanced up, but I saw him hit the key to blank his screen. "What can I do for you?"

Settling into the opposite chair, I said, "That's the question I came in here to ask you. You must have needed someone to do more than juggle a few emails every day."

"Not at the moment. You picked a slow week to start." The soft binging of either an incoming email or some other type of message drew his focus briefly, but he didn't pull his screen back up, and I didn't point out he'd been the one to pick the day I started work.

"Listen, if it's the pay you're worried about, don't. I'm dealing with some outside projects. Nothing is closing in the next week or two. All I need from you is to handle client/underwriter communications, and I don't really care how much of your time it takes or doesn't. Robin has plenty of reading material if you want to hang around, or you can monitor the inbox remotely."

For a guy who had been such a stickler for job history, he seemed pretty lax about the actual job.

"As long as you're on top of getting the information where it needs to be, I don't really care about anything else."

The bing sounded again, and when he gave me a pointed look, I took the hint.

"Okay then. I'm all over it."

But I'd be all over it from anywhere but the office since it was all the same to him. Besides, I still had a few things to do to get settled. Like driving fifteen miles to the nearest center to pick up the cable equipment so I could access the Internet from my laptop, and hitting the hardware store for some paint chips.

The first errand hit a snag right off the bat.

"Yeah, I can give you the set top box and modem, but they're not going to do you any good," said the pleasant-looking man behind the counter. "You don't have a hook up yet."

"I checked your site to see if service was available at my new location, so I'm not sure what the holdup would be."

"Oh, it's available, it's just never been run in from the pole. You're looking at a full install."

Considering she'd lived alone, I was a little suprised Catherine hadn't watched a lot of TV.

"How long before you can get someone to do the install?"

"Probably a week."

Okay, I admit it, I flirted with him, and I did it without the tiniest shred of shame. I'd do it again if I had to, too, because it worked.

“Let me pull up the schedule,” he said with a shy smile. “I’ll see if I can slot you in sooner.”

Five minutes later, I’d gently turned down a date, but had an appointment for my cable to be hooked up by noon the next day. Plus, I’d decided it felt good to be looked at as an attractive woman. In fact, it felt refreshing to be looked at without speculation, since that hadn’t happened to me in at least a week.

I carried the feeling with me all the way back to the hardware store, where it quickly dissipated the minute I walked through the door. I sighed and fought the urge to turn around and leave.

"Hey, Everly. Whatcha doing?"

"Hey, David." The man was like Visa—everywhere I wanted to be. “Just taking a look at some paint colors.” Nothing to see here, move along.

Except he didn’t. “Interior or exterior?”

“I thought I’d start in the kitchen. That paper is a little too busy for my taste.”

He sort of stared at me for a moment, then said, “You can’t really paint over wallpaper. Or you can, but it won’t come out smooth or look as nice as it would on bare walls.”

Helpful as the information was, I really hadn’t been looking for new complications when I went in there. “What do you recommend? Taking the wallpaper down first?” Sounded like a lot more work.

“You could, but those old houses, there might be a bunch of layers, and who knows what the plaster looks like underneath.”

“In other words, I could leave up the paper and not get a smooth finish, or waste a lot of time taking it down and not get a smooth finish.”

Not that I’d seen a lot of it, but he did have a nice grin. “In a nutshell.”

"Well, you've been extra helpful, I must say." While he'd pointed out the folly of the attempt, I'd been picking out paint chips in various shades of yellow, anyhow. Even if the resulting surface looked rough, the reduction of pattern was a good trade-off. "I'm going to go for it anyway."

“Hey, I’ve got to go, but do yourself a favor and buy the heavy-duty primer. You might have to put on a few more coats to get it to cover if you go with the cheaper stuff.”

Left alone, finally, I was reading the instructions on the back of the primer can when I heard a low-voiced conversation in the next aisle.

"Poker game still on for tonight?"

The shelf of paint stood between me and whoever was talking, so I held my breath so I could hear better.

"No, man. Called off on account of the funeral. Scoot wanted to pay his respects. Bandy's going, too. Everyone is, I think."

"Polk says he was killed before midnight, and we played until at least two. You know, if Hudson hadn't let his old lady push him into giving up the game, he'd have been tossing his ante in the kitty instead of himself killed. It woulda only been his wallet taking the hit."

Their voices became fainter, and when I heard footsteps moving away, I hurried to get to where I could see who'd been talking, but didn't make it in time.

If they'd all been playing poker at the time of the murder, I could cross Scooter off the list along with the rest of the poker players, and I wouldn't have to stake out Bandy's to see if I could learn anything.

At this point, I was down to a single suspect: the father of the boy who'd been hurt in the basketball game. Would he show up at the funeral? In a few hours, I'd find out.

If I'd wanted to make an understated entrance to Hudson's funeral, that opportunity went out the window when I walked in with my arm around a pale and shaking Neena for support. Heads turned, eyes widened, and Hudson's mother let out a shriek of protest that her husband tried to muffle.

He, at least, had the decency to give Neena an apologetic smile before leading his wife from the room.

The crowd parted as I escorted the widow toward the open casket, her steps become more labored as we went. About halfway there, solemn-faced, Jacy appeared like an angel to take Neena's other arm, and a hush fell over the crowd.

Knowing Hudson was gone wasn't the same as seeing the concrete proof, and having been cut out of all the decision making or early viewing, I'm sure Neena felt blind-sided by having her first glimpse of him being in public.

Tears ran down my face, and we held her as she looked down at the still face of her beloved. Gently, she patted his hand then leaned down to kiss his cheek. I felt the shudder go through her, but when she stood straight, she whispered, “He’d want me to be strong.”

Shoulders squared, she turned and waited to accept condolences from anyone not too intimidated by Viola to offer them.

She might have been comforted to know Hudson’s ghost stood by her side, his face a grave mask as he observed the grace she showed, even to Viola when that woman took her place near the coffin fifteen minutes or so later.

Viola’s eyes looked a little glassy, and I wondered if her husband had slipped her a sedative. If he did, I applauded his judgment. I didn’t think she and Neena would bond over their loss, but there wouldn’t be a scene, and that was good enough for now.

"I'm okay," Neena whispered to me when I shot her a glance to see how she was holding up. "Don't go far, though."

Knowing it wasn't our place to stand as family, Jacy and I left her there but kept an eye out in case we were needed.

On the plus side, I now had a chance to take a look around at the attendees, and the place was packed.

The baseball team attended in uniform, and among them, looking thinner than on the photo was the boy from the collection box. I intended to keep an eye out for his parents when the service began, and I refocused my attention on Hudson and the tragedy of his loss.

CHAPTER 25

The preacher spoke eloquently of a life taken too soon, and of a man who, at the heart of him, cared about his community. There wasn't a dry eye in the place, and when it was over, most everyone adjourned to the town hall for a potluck dinner in Hudson's honor.

Everyone in town must have donated something, including several containers of meatballs from Bertinos. Jacy and I were alone in the kitchen.

Jacy shook her head in disgust as she looked around the room. "I think half these people only showed up because they wanted to get a look at Neena and chow down on free food. Viola has a few of her cronies convinced she's the killer." She pulled the foil off the top of the disposable pan and tipped the contents into a warming pan.

"Wasn't her, and we both know it. I'm pretty sure I know who it was, though." I lit the burner under the pan while she added more meatballs. "I saw his car at the motel—I just didn't realize it until yesterday."

"Well," she said, turning toward me with brows raised, "don't keep me in suspense."

"It's the father of that kid, the one who—"

A crash sounded from around the corner where the sinks were, and we both about jumped out of our skins. Somebody had bumped into the table and knocked a whole pan of lasagna to the floor. We rushed forward to help clean it up before anybody could fall in it, and by the time we'd finished, a couple acquaintances from high school cornered me to get the scoop firsthand.

I could tell Jacy was about to burst, but it wasn't like we could talk in front of them.

Viola kept her distance from Neena, and whatever poison the woman had tried to spread was dissipated by the widow's gentle demeanor because she was treated warmly and with deference. A fact that had Viola looking like she wanted to chew chain and spit nails.

After the meal, I left her to Jacy's tender care and went to help my mother with some of the cleaning up while folks took turns telling stories about Hudson. That was how I came to learn my latest theory held less water than a thimble.

Yes, the boy with cancer had been hurt during basketball practice, but the injury for which Hudson was demoted had turned out to be a blessing in disguise. During the scan to rule out a concussion, the radiologist found signs of cancer, and only by early detection had Bobby's disease become known. The intense headache he'd had from playing the game had saved the teen's life.

Another motive shot to hell.

And so, I was at ground zero again that evening when my doorbell rang unexpectedly, and I saw Ray the pizza guy on the front steps. I hadn't ordered pizza, but I figured Jacy had sent him along as one of her *taking care of a friend* gestures, and I was grateful.

"Hey," I said when he stepped inside. "I'm glad to see you, but I didn't order anything."

He closed the door behind him, and I got a glimpse at the look on his face.

"Oh, I think you did. You've been meddling."

The pizza box hit the floor, and I knew I was in trouble when I saw the knife in his hand. My body went hot as fire.

"Ray, you don't want to do this." Keep him talking was all I could think to do. Maybe I could convince him to put the knife down.

"You don't know what I want, but I'll tell you. My kid is going to go to Louisiana State, and he's going to play ball, and he's going to get signed to a major franchise. That's what I want, and I'll do whatever it takes to make that happen." A few expressions flitted across his face: anger, sorrow, regret. "I just went there to talk to Hudson that night, make him see reason. He wouldn't though, and I lost it for a minute." He cast his eyes down for a second. "Before I even knowed what was happenin', he was dead."

I looked around for something, anything, to defend myself with, while trying to figure out how I'd come onto his radar. "How is killing me going to help?"

"I know you figured out it was me who done Hudson. I heard you tell that other girl at the funeral, and I can't let you ruin my family. My boy'd never live it down." Fire lit his eyes again. "This is all Hudson's fault. Put my kid on the bench because of a science test. Kid with an arm like my boy, he don't need no science anyway. But you don't pull your best shot at a win out of the game when there's a college scout watching."

I shook my head. "You're not even who I was talking about. But even so, there's no proof you did it, Ray. You can walk away right now, and no one will ever know. Even if I did go to the police, there's no evidence, and Ernie already thinks I'm an idiot, so he'd never believe me." Slowly I edged toward the parlor door. Maybe he'd get distracted, and I could shoot inside and lock him out.

"Ev." Hudson's voice sounded loud in my ear, and I felt the cool ice of him there. "I'm here. Whatever happens, you're not alone."

"Might as well be," I muttered.

Ray took a step and closed some of the distance between us. He meant to kill me, I could see that in his eyes plain enough, but there was a part of him that regretted the necessity.

"What would your son say if he knew what you'd done? You say you don't want his life ruined, but how are you going to look at him even if you do get away with it, which you won't. No way will you get away with two murders, and when he finds out, he'll lose all respect for you. And the other kids will ostracize him."

"Kids don't know what's best for them." As he took another menacing step, Hudson shot an arm through Ray's head and the man flinched. Hard. So Hudson followed with a gut punch and then appeared to grasp the wrist holding the knife. Even though his hand passed right through, the sensation must have disoriented him.

For a moment, I thought we'd won. Ray dropped the knife. I darted forward and gave it a kick that sent the weapon shooting across the floor and under the locked closet door. Now, it was just Ray and me.

Undeterred by the loss of the knife or by Hudson's repeated blows, Ray advanced again, and I found myself grappling with the man. He smelled of oregano and garlic. We struggled while Hudson howled out his anger, and then I felt Ray's hands on my throat.

He had me against the door, and I couldn't breathe. He was going to kill me after all. The last thing I'd see before I died would be the face of a maniac, and Hudson staring at me over his shoulder. As the thought flitted through my head, Hudson disappeared, and I heard a commotion at the top of the stairs.

With what little strength I had left, I tried to ram a knee into Ray's tender bits, but he held me too tightly. My vision started to go blurry and gray, and then I saw the impossible.

"What the—" Ray turned to look over his shoulder just as a mannequin head launched off the upper landing, bounced down the stairs and hit him in the side of the head.

"Strike," Hudson yelled from somewhere above me. The big man went down like a set of bowling pins, the pressure on my throat was gone.

I pulled in one burning breath, and then another.

"Is he dead?" Hudson wanted to know as he hovered over Ray's prone body.

His chest rose and fell even though the rest of him remained motionless, and I shook my head. "Just knocked out."

"Well, you'd better call Ernie, but first tie him up or something, just in case he wakes up. He's not gonna be out for long."

It was good advice, so I grabbed a tie-back from the parlor drapes and did just that. "Thanks for saving me. But what am I supposed to tell Ernie when he gets here? I don't think he's going to believe me if I say you were here and played a round of ghost bowling-for-killers with a mannequin head."

In the end, Ernie had no choice but to accept my story that the upstairs closet had been open and in a freak turn of events, a mannequin head had rolled down from the top of the pile, banked off the wall, and rocketed down the stairs to peg Ray Watson at just the right moment. It was a far stretch for sure but was the best I could come up with on the spur of the moment.

When he came to, Ray not only corroborated my story but confessed to killing Hudson after being turned down for a second mortgage on his house. He'd needed his son to get a scholarship, and the only way was for Tony to play in the game. Since Hudson had been reinstated as head coach, something not even Neena had known, he'd stuck tight to the rules. Tony's science grade dipped, and Hudson had to bench him.

With Hudson out of the way, a crisp hundred dollar bill to the interim coach secured Tony's place on the pitching mound for the pivotal game. Another got him a post-game makeup test, and as far as Ray was concerned, he'd done his best by his son.

I took no lasting damage from my encounter with a mad man, and after Ernie slapped the cuffs on Ray, Hudson made me renew my promise to watch out for Neena before he said his final goodbye. I watched him go into the light with mixed emotions, and sincerely hoped he would be my one and only ghostly encounter.

Grammie Dupree, in all her wisdom, had a saying about wishes and horses, though, and she hadn't been wrong yet.

EPILOGUE

Thursday morning, I swung through the office door feeling refreshed and ready to take on the day until I got a look at Robin's normally bland face. Was that an actual expression she was wearing?

"You've got a problem," she informed me without preamble.

Steeling myself, I waited for her to elaborate, and when she didn't, I resorting to asking her to explain.

"They moved up the closing date for 27 Front Street, and Spencer's not answering his phone. You're going to have to take the paperwork over and stay for the signing.

Oh no, I would not.

"You know I can't do that, I'm not licensed. Shoot the info to my email, and I'll see what I can do about rescheduling. Does this kind of thing happen a lot?" Given how lax my new employer was about my hours, I wondered about job stability. Well, that and he'd asked me to tell one of the more difficult cases that he had funding in place when underwriting had not verified 100%. I wasn't too happy to lie to an applicant when he'd been stringing her along for months already even if he was certain he could get the deal through. It didn't seem fair.

"Never. Spence wouldn't miss a signing, and he'd been pulling in favors to get this one done early, but it didn't look like it was going to happen."

I wanted to ask why she hadn't made the calls herself, but then I was the assistant and she was mostly part of the decor, so I handled the situation the best I could. Spencer still hadn't shown up by the time I was done, and he didn't call or answer his phone as I readied myself to leave an hour later with my emails caught up for the morning.

Just before I shut off my computer, someone from Patrea Heard's office called and asked me to come in on Monday, but refused to give me any more information.

It looked like week two post-life apocalypse might also be starting out with a bang.

Made in the USA
Coppell, TX
28 January 2021